Debbie whispered.

"Quiet!"

"But it's true, isn't it? It's always been there—for both of us—from the first moment."

"You flatter yourself."

"You're a coward, Jake," she murmured against his mouth. "You can't face the truth."

Hell might freeze over but no one could call Jake Garfield a coward. With one swift movement he lifted her in his arms and held her tight, her face close to his. "Take that back," he commanded.

She regarded him with impish defiance. "Make me."

Dear Reader,

Are you looking for books that are fresh, sexy and wonderfully romantic? Then look no more, because you've got one of them in your hands right now! Silhouette Desire, where man meets woman...

Starting this month's selection is Dixie Browning's *Man of the Month,* Alex Hightower, the first hero in Dixie's new mini-series, TALL, DARK AND HANDSOME. He's got *three* women on his mind...

Then Ryanne Corey gives us a love-and-laughter tonic by showing us what could happen when a perfectly normal woman gets pushed to the limits and goes wild! Picking up Tray Malone might have been a bit too daring though!

Daring and dangerous are adjectives that fit Mitch Ryan well. He's THE SAINT OF BOURBON STREET, and the second of BJ James's MEN OF THE BLACK WATCH. Look for Matthew's book next month to finish off the trilogy.

There are also three terrific novels from Lucy Gordon, Susan Crosby and Judith McWilliams, so make sure you don't miss any of them!

Happy reading!

The Editor

Two-Faced Woman
LUCY GORDON

SILHOUETTE

Desire

All the characters in this book have no existence outside the imagination
of the author, and have no relation whatsoever to anyone bearing the
same name or names. They are not even distantly inspired by any
individual known or unknown to the author, and all the incidents are pure
invention.

First published in Great Britain 1996
by Silhouette Books, Eton House, 18-24 Paradise Road,
Richmond, Surrey TW9 1SR

© Lucy Gordon 1995

Silhouette, Silhouette Desire and Colophon are
Trade Marks of Harlequin Enterprises II B.V.

ISBN 0 373 05953 1

22-9602

Made and printed in Great Britain

LUCY GORDON

met her husband-to-be in Venice, fell in love the first evening and got engaged two days later. Many years later, they're still happily married and now live in England with their three dogs. For twelve years Lucy was a writer for an English women's magazine. She interviewed many of the world's most interesting men, including Warren Beatty, Richard Chamberlain, Sir Roger Moore, Sir Alec Guinness and Sir John Gielgud.

Other Silhouette Books by Lucy Gordon

Silhouette Special Edition

Legacy of Fire
Enchantment in Venice
Bought Woman
Outcast Woman
Seduced by Innocence

Silhouette Desire

Take All Myself
The Judgement of Paris
A Coldhearted Man
My Only Love, My Only Hate
A Fragile Beauty
Just Good Friends
Eagle's Prey
For Love Alone
Vengeance is Mine
Convicted of Love
The Sicilian
On His Honour
Married in Haste
Uncaged

One

Debbie Harker strode into the hotel room without knocking. The man inside looked up quickly. He was middle-aged and wore a perpetually alarmed expression, which deepened when he saw her. "I'm just checking that everything's all right, ma'am," he said hastily.

"No need to call me 'ma'am,' George," Debbie told him, tossing her purse onto the bed and moving around to study the room. She had a brisk, purposeful manner that instantly dominated her surroundings and her companion. "I'm not in the police anymore. I'm a private investigator now."

"Yeah, so you told me on the phone. You could have knocked me down with a feather when you said you wanted to hire me to take some photographs." George became awkward. "After all, you know my specialty..."

"Rude pictures," Debbie confirmed.

"Artistic studies," George tried to protest.

"Knock it off, George. I've seen your work, remember. That's why I had to ask you to recommend a venue. I want some pics that will place a gentleman in a very awkward situation."

George's alarm deepened. "You mean, blackmail?"

"In a way. We're going to blackmail a blackmailer, a nasty piece of work called Elroy Speke. He specializes in women who did a bit of nude modeling when they were young but have put it behind them now. Speke buys up the old pictures and threatens to publish them. My client is one of those women. I aim to put a stop to his little game once and for all. Are you sure this place is suitably equipped?"

"Perfect. That mirror behind you is two-way. My stuff is on the other side."

Debbie regarded the large mirror on the front of the wardrobe. From this side it looked perfectly normal, but George showed her the inside of the wardrobe that was actually a tiny, concealed room where his camera had been set up. Debbie stepped inside and closed the door. She found she had a good view of the bedroom, which was comfortable in an anonymous fashion. Apart from the double bed there was a wardrobe, a table, a small refrigerator and an armchair. The tones of the carpet, curtains and bedspread were variations of brown and biscuit, and there were no ornaments anywhere.

She stepped back into the bedroom and glanced out of the window, enjoying the sense of anticipation that a difficult job always gave her. It was a longing for that heady sense of excitement that had made her join the police force ten years ago, at the age of eighteen. But she'd soon found that police work had its share of dull routine. She'd climbed the ladder as far as detective sergeant, where her propensity to ditch routine in favor of inspiration had made her superiors tear their hair out.

"And just who the hell are you to chuck the book aside whenever it suits you?" Chief Superintendent Manners, her mentor and guide, had bawled. "The book is there for a reason."

"If I'd stuck to the book you wouldn't have Slasher Gibbs in the cells now," she retorted with spirit.

"No, and I wouldn't have the chief commissioner breathing down my neck about your unorthodox methods, either. Detective Sergeant Harker, this is your last chance. I'm taking you off the streets and putting you behind a desk until you cool down."

Debbie set her chin. "I didn't join the force to do paperwork, *sir.*"

Manners breathed hard and his face turned a dangerous puce. "You will do paperwork if I say so. *Is that clear?*"

"Yes, sir. And I quit."

She left that day and set up in business as a private investigator. In six months she'd enjoyed some modest success, helped along by a few crumbs sent her way by Manners. But this was her most challenging assignment yet and she was looking forward to it.

Despite her confident manner she'd experienced a few initial qualms about going in for blackmail. But after hearing Jane Quinlan's full story she had no doubt that right was on her side. "I was nineteen years old when I posed for those damned pictures," Jane had told her in despair. "I was a student. I needed money for food and to pay the rent."

She'd gone on to make a successful career as a lawyer and was now preparing for her marriage to a prominent politician. But the news of her engagement had brought

Elroy Speke crawling out of the woodwork, flourishing photographs that Jane had long forgotten about.

"I've tried offering him money," Jane said wretchedly. "But he's not interested. He wants 'favors.'"

They'd been sitting in the cubbyhole Debbie called her office. It was just big enough for a table, two chairs and a coffee percolator. Debbie filled another cup and offered it to Jane. "You mean, he's such a worm that he can't get women any other way?" she asked.

"No, it's not that. If he wasn't such a rat I'd say he's quite good-looking. But he seems to get his kicks from women who are afraid of him. Also, I think he's trying to revenge himself on his wife."

"What's he got against her?"

"She's rolling in money and he hasn't a penny of his own. He's got a flashy car, plus a wardrobe full of silk shirts and handmade shoes, and she paid for the lot. He hates being dependent but he hasn't got the guts to walk out and live off his own wits. So he 'evens the score' by using her money to buy these pictures and then sleep with his victims."

"You mean, she knows?"

"Goodness, no. He gets back at her in his head. She'd chuck him out like a shot if she found out."

"Then why not tell her?"

"I threatened to. Speke just laughed and said, 'Prove it. It's your word against mine.' And he's right."

"Then we have to get some proof that he can't deny," Debbie had said thoughtfully. "And there's really only one way to do it."

So the plan was born. Debbie had contacted Elroy Speke, offered him a set of "very interesting pictures," and asked him to meet her at a discreet hotel in a quiet part of London. She'd gotten the name of the hotel from

George, who was a mine field of information about dubious premises. Now there was nothing to do but wait.

"When will she get here?" George asked.

"She? Who?"

"Well, you've got a stripper to set him up, haven't you? Off with her clothes, into the fancy poses, that kind of thing."

"The 'stripper' is me, George."

George's jaw dropped. "You're going to do it yourself?"

"I thought the fewer people involved, the better."

"But do you know what you're doing?" he demanded with outraged professionalism. "It's an art, you know. It ain't just taking your clothes off any old how."

"I know that. I've had a lesson from one of your own models. What's the matter? Don't you think I'm up to the job?"

She laughed as she said it for she knew that she brought first-class equipment to the task. She was five feet nine inches tall and slim but curved. Her pale, almost silvery blond hair added a touch of glamour. She wore a short, tight, black leather skirt, and a black leather jacket that was designed to be provocative. It was skintight, emphasizing the swell of her breasts and her tiny waist. There were no sleeves and the shoulders were cut away almost to the neck, but the neck itself was high and the edges kept in place by a zipper. "Yes—No—Try your luck!" That was the message that it sent. Debbie knew she looked dramatically effective, and when George regarded her with a critical eye she met his gaze unafraid. "You've got some very nice assets there," he said at last, judicially. "If you ever need to earn a bit extra—"

"Cut it out, George," she told him with a chuckle. "Save the spiel for someone who doesn't know you as well as I do."

He sighed. "Can't blame me for trying. What about this bloke? Is he photogenic?"

"No idea. My client didn't have a picture of him. She says he's tall and dark, late thirties. I've given him a description of myself. As far as he knows I'm called Esther Bridges." She checked her watch. "I'm meeting him downstairs. If you're sure everything's all right here, I'll go down and wait."

"I'll put some music on," George suggested. "I've got a very quiet camera, but a little extra noise doesn't hurt."

It was twenty minutes before Speke was due but she preferred to be there early. It was part of being on top of the job. And she was glad she'd done it when after five minutes a sleek sports car drew up outside the hotel and a tall, dark man in his late thirties leapt out. Debbie's soul burned at the sight of that car. She knew how much it cost. She'd sighed over it, yearned for it, twisted her budget every which way in a fruitless attempt to convince herself that she could afford that high-priced beauty. And this man had bought it with money from the wife he was deceiving.

But none of this appeared on her face. She was regarding the door with a cool expression as Speke strode into the hotel lobby. He glanced around and met her eye. There was a question in his face and his eyebrows lifted slightly. She answered with a nod and sauntered forward. "I believe I'm the person you've come to see?" she said.

"If you've got something for me, then you're the person I've come to see," he agreed.

"Oh, yes," she said sweetly. "I've got something for you, something you're really going to like."

"Well?" he said impatiently.

"You don't expect me to have it down here, surely? It's upstairs in my room."

"Then let's go and get it."

Debbie led the way upstairs, concealing her surprise. He wasn't exactly as she'd expected. The car fitted Jane's picture, but apart from his shoes, his clothes didn't. As Jane had said, the shoes were handmade and, like the car, they gleamed with costly quality. But everything else about his looks took her aback. He wore old jeans and a leather jacket that might have been expensive when it was new, but that was a long time ago. Nor did he have any of the smooth charm of the con man. His manner was rough and almost irritable. But perhaps that was his method, she reflected. Maybe smooth charm was a played-out commodity and he'd calculated that roughness looked more like sincerity.

But in one thing Speke fitted her mental picture. He was as attractive as Jane had suggested, with lean features that might have been almost too handsome if they hadn't become weather-beaten along the way. His voice had a melodious bass beauty that had given her a shock, and beneath the shabby clothing his body had a powerful athleticism that nothing could hide.

The room was empty as she led him in. Cool, sultry modern jazz came from the radio. Debbie didn't even glance at the mirror. All her attention was focused on what she was about to do. "Let me get you a drink," she offered, swaying over to the refrigerator.

"No, thank you," he said. "I don't have much time. You know what I came for. Why don't we get straight down to business?"

"Because there are things we haven't discussed yet," she said in a soft, husky voice that was calculated to melt his bones. "Besides, you don't mind spending a little time with me, do you?"

He opened his mouth as if to argue, then something seemed to arrest his attention. Debbie was surveying him in a languid manner that was full of invitation, and a smile just touched her curved lips. "That might be—interesting," he agreed.

"Oh, I'm a very interesting woman," she promised. "Wouldn't you like to find out just how interesting I can be?"

His eyes narrowed. "Is this how you normally do business?"

"That depends on who I'm doing business with. With some people I take more trouble than others."

The corner of his mouth quirked. It wasn't a smile exactly, certainly not a friendly smile. There was something wary and suspicious about it, but it also made his face disconcertingly attractive. "And you plan to take trouble with me?" he queried.

"I think I'll enjoy taking trouble with you," she agreed. "Don't you find it a little hot in here? Why don't you take this off?" She indicated his jacket, and he didn't resist when she slipped it off his shoulders. "That's better," she purred.

He put his head on one side and regarded her cynically. "I guess the next step is for you to take something off?" he suggested.

She gave him a wide-eyed gaze. "Do you think I should?"

"I think you should do whatever you want," he told her. "This is your party. I'm just fascinated to see how it's going to develop."

Without answering, Debbie began to pull down the zipper that secured the tight leather jacket. Her companion didn't move a muscle as it went lower and lower, but she could hear the soft rasp of his breathing that had suddenly grown faster. His eyes were fixed on her as her pale, silky skin came into view inch by inch. At last she shrugged off the jacket, revealing beautiful breasts, barely confined in a wispy black lace bra. She smiled at him with confidence. She knew her body was beautiful.

She was swaying in time to the music now, infusing her movements with a sensuous, erotic grace that she could see was having its effect. Her companion was watching her, riveted, and the jeering smile had died on his lips. She unfastened her skirt and let that, too, slip to the ground. She wore no tights beneath it, only skimpy black panties that matched the bra. She pushed her fingers up into her pale blond hair and let her head fall back as she sashayed about the room in time to the music. The movements were intended to suggest ecstasy and display her shape to the fullest advantage.

"Now, what about you?" she murmured, beginning to finger the buttons of his shirt.

He closed one hand over hers. "Before we go any further, there's something we should get straight," he said in a husky voice.

"What's that?"

"I don't play games, and I won't stand for a woman playing games with me. Do you understand me?"

Now she could believe that he was a ruthless blackmailer, for there was hard intent in his eyes that boded ill for his enemies. A man without a heart, she thought, capable of anything.

"Do you understand me?" he repeated. "If you turn out to be a tease, you'll be sorry."

There was something merciless about him that almost made Debbie afraid. His hand held hers in a light grip, yet through it she could feel sinews of steel and a strength that owed as much to nerves as to muscle. For the first time she wondered if she was wise to arouse passions she had no intention of satisfying. But there was no turning back now. She'd given her word to a client and she wasn't a quitter. When it came to putting him off, she'd just have to rely on the self-defense techniques she'd learned on the force.

"Why do you talk so much?" she purred. "There are so many more interesting ways of spending our time."

He released her hand. "Just as long as we understand each other."

Button by button his shirt came undone. His chest was smooth and lean, positively inviting her to run her fingers over it. She accepted the invitation, and received a shock of pleasure at the feel of his firm flesh. "Why don't you take your shirt right off?" she murmured.

"Why don't you do it for me?" he asked with a grin.

She tossed the shirt aside. At once she felt his arm snake around her waist, drawing her close so that her almost-naked body was pressed against his bare chest. "Do you read your stars?" he asked.

"I—well, no—" she managed to answer. To her dismay and annoyance she sounded confused, but that was nothing to how she felt. The feel of being held close to him was disturbingly thrilling.

"You should," he assured her. "I read mine every day. This morning they said I was going to have a wonderful surprise. And they were right." He put his other hand beneath her neck, holding her while he dropped his head to brush his lips against the line of her jaw. Debbie set her teeth, trying not to gasp out loud. His mouth had touched her only lightly, but that was enough to send sparks of fire glittering through her. While she tried to fight her reaction he did it again, letting his lips linger this time before trailing them slowly down her neck. The sensation was so poignantly pleasurable that she clutched her hair. Her mind was telling her to end this now but her body was urging her to throw back her head in abandon.

It was all wrong, she told herself frantically. Everything she knew about this man was bad, but that seemed to have faded to the back of her consciousness. The front was occupied by the frenzy of pleasure that was making its way inexorably through her.

Fighting to collect her wits, she began to work on the fastening of his trousers. She needed him as nearly naked as possible, then George could get his pictures and she could bring this to an end. But she didn't want it to end. As she cast his trousers away she yielded to the temptation to run her hands over his flanks, enjoying the discovery of their lean tautness and the sense of power ready to spring. There was power in his arms, too, as they drew her down onto the bed and pressed her back against the pillows, propping himself on elbows to look down at her. "You're a very beautiful woman," he said.

Suddenly she couldn't speak. His closeness and the sensations coursing through her had caused a constriction in her throat. If he discovered that, he'd know she was losing control and that would be fatal. So instead she smiled at him, slowly, enticingly. She didn't know it but that smile was full of the mad pleasure that was pounding in her veins. Her chest rose and fell with the rhythm of desire that had begun to beat insistently through her. He looked down at her breasts, softly moving against him, barely covered by the tiny bra. He slid his fingers inside and gave the flimsy item a quick jerk that destroyed it. He tossed the pieces into a corner and enveloped one breast in a shapely hand, letting the ball of his thumb rasp across the nipple.

Debbie gasped at the poignant sensation, and flung her hands out. But instead of pushing him away she found she was clinging on to him, running her fingers through his springy hair. She just managed to suppress a groan. Nothing in her life had felt as good as that. He repeated the action more slowly, and although she choked back the gasp of pleasure, she couldn't control her body, which had developed a life of its own. It arched instinctively against him, reveling in the contact of their skin and the soft friction as she moved against him. Her arms wound around him of their own accord, pulling him closer. He paused a moment to look searchingly into her face. Then, with tantalizing slowness, he lowered his head and laid his mouth on hers.

It was as though a flaming torch had touched her mouth. In the very first moment she knew that this was more than a kiss. It was a baptism of fire, and she was ready, eager for it. One tiny part of her mind, that was still professional, found time to hope that George was getting all this. The next moment all common sense was engulfed in the flames of excitement that were consuming her. His lips were hard, determined, seeking, intruding, commanding and enticing all at the same time.

His hands were at work all over her body, touching, teasing, thrilling. They were like no other man's hands had ever been, possessing the skill of the devil, knowing how to drive a woman to madness. She'd meant to half seduce him, keep everything under control and bring matters coolly to a conclusion when it suited her. But all that was slipping away now. She had no control left, only the yearning for this to go on, never stopping until it reached the perfect conclusion.

Her blood thrummed in her veins as she thought of that conclusion. Some distant corner of her brain, where sanity still lived, shouted a desperate warning. This was a bad character, a criminal—apart from that, he was a total stranger to her and she had no right to be naked in his arms. But her body knew better. Her flesh sang and told her that this was the man she'd been made for, and he'd been too long finding her. It was monstrous, crazy— and inevitable.

His face was before her eyes, and now she saw that the look of cool cynicism was gone and he was as thunderstruck as she. He, too, was caught up in something that made a mockery of calculation, and which could have only one appointed end.

Then a shudder went through him and he seemed to control himself by sheer force. "Well?" he rasped. A pulse was twitching near his jaw and his whole body seemed to be made of steel. Debbie could feel him fighting to master his own desire while he eyed her narrowly.

"Well?" she gasped.

"Are you ready to go through with it?"

She looked at him wildly. Was she ready? Was she crazy? This was a man whose control over himself was awesome, terrifying. Could she match it, or would she yield to the wild thrumming in her blood, the craving need in her loins to feel him there?

"Answer me," he said in a voice that was almost a snarl.

She drew a long, shaky breath. "I—"

But before she could say more there was a crash from inside the wardrobe. Debbie turned wild eyes toward it and saw the door swing open, revealing George sitting on the wardrobe floor, tangled up in the legs of his tripod. The man also looked at him sharply, uttered a profanity, and began to rise. Quick as a flash Debbie tightened her arms about him. For a few mad moments they struggled, he trying to get free, she restraining him, while George frantically grabbed his gear and headed for the door. At last the man's greater strength prevailed, but Debbie had delayed him just long enough to give George a head start. As the door slammed behind the terrified photographer the man raced across the floor in pursuit, but Debbie launched herself after him and brought him down with a flying rugby tackle. Her advantage lasted only a moment. With a swiveling movement of his entire body he managed to get on top of her, seizing her wrists and holding them above her head. For a long moment they gazed at each other, breathless, angry, infuriated by their own desire.

"It's too late," Debbie said, gasping. "You won't catch him now."

"You made very sure of that," he said grimly. "And you're going to be sorry that you did."

"I don't think so. I think it's you that's going to be sorry. How would you like those pictures to go to your wife?"

"I don't have a wife."

"Don't try to fool me. I know you're married and you live off her. But the game's up, Mr. Speke—"

"What nonsense are you talking?" he demanded. "My name isn't Speke and I don't have a wife. My name is Jake Garfield, *Detective Inspector* Jake Garfield. And you're under arrest."

Two

"Arrest? What do you mean, arrest?"

"You know what arrest means, Miss James. I doubt if it's the first time you've been behind bars." He leaned back and pulled her up, still holding her wrists. "Elizabeth James, I arrest you on a charge of obstructing a police officer in the course of his duty, of attempted blackmail, and anything else I can think of when I get my clothes on. Whatever you say may be taken down and given in evidence."

Some of the horrible truth was getting through to Debbie. "You're a policeman?" she demanded, aghast.

"Come on, save the wide-eyed innocence. It doesn't go with the performance you've just been putting on. You lured me here on the promise of information and then tried to set me up for blackmail."

"Not you," she managed to say. "Elroy Speke."

"Who the hell is Elroy Speke?"

"You are—aren't you?"

"I've already told you who I am, and my colleagues at the station will be delighted to confirm it. Then you can have a long session in a cell telling yourself it's true," he informed her grimly.

True? Of course it was true! It was all so obvious now that this authoritative man could never be the miserable worm she was after. Her instincts had told her that from the first, but she hadn't listened to them. Now she'd failed in her job and gotten herself arrested into the bargain. Oh, what a mess!

"Will you kindly release me so that I can get dressed?" she asked through gritted teeth.

"Modesty now, is it? I don't recall that modesty was much in evidence when you were inviting me to have an interesting time." But he loosened his grip and got on with his own dressing, taking care to keep between her and the door.

Debbie grabbed frantically at her clothes. The bra was beyond repair so she stuffed it into her purse and fastened the leather jacket up to the neck. Now the shortness of the skirt horrified her and she tried to pull it down, but it was no use. The skirt had been designed for provocation, and provocative it remained. "Why do you keep calling me 'Miss James'?" she asked.

He groaned. "Surely we're past that stage? Why go on pretending?"

"I'm not pretending. I don't know anyone called Elizabeth James. My name is Debra Harker, *ex-Detective Sergeant* Harker. I left the force to become a private investigator. I'm on a case. Now, who are you?"

"All right. We'll play the game to the finish. I'm Detective Inspector Jake Garfield, and *you* are Elizabeth

James. Pretending to be a policewoman was a neat idea
but—''

"There are a dozen people on the force who can tell you
who I am," she interrupted in exasperation. "Starting
with Chief Superintendent Manners."

"Manners?" He looked at her curiously. "Now that
you mention it, I *have* heard Manners bellyaching about
a Debbie Harker on his staff—wild woman, pain in the
neck."

"That's me," Debbie said without hesitation.

Jake studied her through narrowed eyes. "I had a
meeting set up with Liz James who was going to spill the
beans about a nasty character called Lucky Driver. All I
know about her appearance is that she's blond, and they
don't come much blonder than you. You really expect me
to believe you're not her?"

"That's right. Because I'm not."

Jake drew a sharp breath and snatched up the telephone and called the desk. "Is there a young woman with
fair hair waiting down there?" he barked.

Debbie could just hear the male receptionist's voice.
"There was someone answering that description but she's
gone now. If you're Mr. Garfield, she left you a verbal
message."

"I'm Garfield. What did she say?"

The receptionist cleared his throat awkwardly and repeated the message. It was extremely vulgar, very ex-
plicit, and left no doubt that Jake would be wasting his
time trying that source of information again. Jake swore
and slammed down the phone. "Now see what your in-
terference has done!" he snapped.

"Just a minute," Debbie muttered, and seized the
phone in her turn. "Hello, reception? This is Room 18.
Has a Mr. Speke been asking for me?"

"No, madame."

"Are you sure?"

"There's been only a young lady and she's gone."

"Thank you." She replaced the receiver, chagrined.

"So much for Mr. Speke," Jake said ironically.

"He exists. He's making my client's life a misery."

"So you were going to strip off by way of persuading him to stop?"

Debbie ground her teeth. "He's a blackmailer—"

"*He's* a blackmailer?" Jake demanded with angry hilarity.

"I was trying to compromise him to get him to stop his nasty activities but you fouled it all up."

"*I*— Now wait! *You* approached *me* in the lobby, not the other way around. There were no names. You just assumed—on no evidence whatever—that I was Speke."

"Not 'on no evidence.' There was the way you looked at me, raising your eyebrows."

"*Raising*—"

"As if you were asking me if I was the right person."

"I *was* asking if you were the right person. But you weren't."

"How was I supposed to know that? And then there was your car. It's a rich man's car."

"No need to tell me that. I live in poverty just to keep up the repayments."

"You're not too poor to afford handmade shoes."

"I have bad feet," he said through gritted teeth. "I *need* handmade shoes. So that's enough to convict me of blackmail, is it? I wish I could sit through one of your cases in court. It must be interesting."

"You played along," she said indignantly. "You didn't use any names, either, and you didn't try to stop me stripping off."

"I was fascinated to know how far you were ready to go."

"Oh, yes?"

"And I was riveted by the performance, I don't deny. You have some very special skills there. In fact..." He stopped and looked at her speculatively. "Very special," he repeated slowly. "So special, in fact, that you might be the one woman I need."

"What are you talking about?"

"Let's assume that you really are ex-policewoman Debbie Harker. I'm not convinced but I'm willing to give you the benefit of the doubt."

"You're so kind," she murmured ironically.

"Once you worked on the side of the law, but who knows whose side you're on now?"

"Hey—"

"Let's say that you've had no success as a P.I.—a reasonable assumption after today's fiasco. Let's say that you're desperate, that you'll take any job without asking too many questions."

"No, let's not say that," she said angrily. "Because it isn't true."

"So you claim. But suppose you were sent here by Lucky Driver, who maybe suspected that his girlfriend might be about to rat on him? Your job was to distract me so that she never got the chance to talk."

"Rubbish," Debbie said trenchantly. "If he thought that, it would be simpler for him to prevent her coming here at all. You don't believe a word you've just said."

"You miss the point, Miss Harker. I could *choose* to believe it, thus giving myself an excuse to dump you in the cells. Couldn't I?"

"If you want to be unpleasant about this, yes."

"But I *am* unpleasant," he informed her affably. "Ask around. You won't find anyone with a good word to say for me. And I don't just mean the crooks."

"I believe it."

"So the question is, what are you going to do to convince me that you're on the side of the angels?"

"Sock you in the jaw," she said darkly.

He grinned. "Don't try it. You caught me by surprise with that rugby tackle, but I'm on guard now. You wrecked a good case, but I'm going to be reasonable about it because you can be useful to me."

"Suppose I don't want to be useful to you?" she demanded crossly.

"Let's say it's in your own interests to convince me that you're who and what you say you are."

His eyes were hard and uncompromising. Debbie faced him defiantly, but she knew that he held the high cards. "So how am I going to be useful?"

"I need a woman to work undercover with me."

"There are plenty of policewomen for that."

"None who are suitable. This job requires special skills, the kind you've proved you have in abundance. Do you know Lucky's Place?"

"I've heard of it. It's a nightclub. Very glitzy and expensive."

"It's also a gambling establishment where a great deal of money gets lost and won. The perfect laundering setup for drug money, and probably a drug distribution center."

"Is that how it's being used?"

"I'm sure of it. The key lies with the man who owns and runs it, Abel Driver, known to his friends and enemies as 'Lucky.' He's a crook who uses the nightclub as a cover for crime, but proving it is another matter. I plan to get a job on the inside, but that's not enough. Lucky has a weakness for women. You can get closer to him than I ever could. It's no use hoping for anything from Liz. She'll be on the run by now, if she's got any sense.''

''Aren't you forgetting something?''

''I don't think so. What?''

''My professional pride.''

''Your what?'' he asked hilariously.

''My professional pride,'' she repeated through gritted teeth. ''I happen to be on a case at the moment. You may think it's just a big joke—''

''If you conduct them all as you did today I think I'll die laughing,'' he retorted without any sign of amusement whatsoever.

She resisted the temptation to toss her drink over him. ''I'm on a case,'' she repeated. ''I can't undertake another job until Elroy Speke is stopped.''

''Are you out of your mind? You've blown your own case as thoroughly as you've blown mine.''

''Then you'll have to help me with him, won't you?''

''*What?* Do you think I've got nothing better to do than pick up the pieces after your mistakes?''

''Not at the moment you haven't, because without my help you can't pursue Lucky Driver.''

''And I'm going to have your help—if you know what's good for you.''

Debbie gave him a sudden mischievous smile that brought a tremor of remembered enchantment to his loins and a scowl to his face. ''Oh, I'll help you, Detective Inspector,'' she declared with a theatrical emphasis that warned him something was coming. ''At least, I'll do my very best. But I can't promise how good my best will be when I'm so *worried* about Elroy Speke and my poor client...''

"Somebody should have strangled you at birth," he growled.

"Will you help me neutralize Speke?"

"I'll do better than that. I'll neutralize him myself, without any help from you. That way I can be sure there won't be any foul-ups."

"Thank you."

"Don't mention it!"

"I won't."

"Now all that remains is for you to tell me where I can get hold of your photographer."

"What do you want him for?"

"Because I'm not going to stand for that kind of picture of me on the open market. I'm going to get his pictures and then I'm going to put the fear of God into him. Now, who is he and where do I find him?"

"I never betray a source."

"You'll betray this one."

"Like hell I will." Debbie set her chin, her eyes glinting with defiance.

After a moment Jake shrugged. He could recognize mulelike stubbornness when he saw it, and there was no point in fighting about this when his contacts would probably enable him to track the man down. He'd gotten a reasonable look at him. "Give me your address," he said. "I'll be in touch when I'm ready." He took the paper she handed him and said, "Cancel anything else you have on hand and hold yourself in readiness."

Debbie gritted her teeth. "I can see why you're so popular."

"I never wasted time on popularity, Miss Harker. It never put anyone behind bars. Now, let's get out of here. I'm busy if you're not."

He walked out of the hotel bedroom, forcing her to follow. "You're a real charmer, aren't you?" she said scathingly.

For answer, he turned so that she was forced to back against the wall. "You've only just got a glimpse of how charming I can be. There'll be others—"

"Hey..." she said suddenly, for she'd seen something over his shoulder.

"Just a moment, I haven't finished."

"But there's—"

"Be quiet and listen. I don't want to work with you because, frankly, your working methods aren't impressive, but circumstances are going to force it on me. But let's set the ground rules. I give the orders and you take them. Is that clear?"

"Perfectly, *mon capitane!*" She saluted ironically.

"Are you trying to be funny?" he asked coldly.

"Would you know the difference?"

"Don't push me, Miss Harker."

"Then don't lecture me about your brilliant methods. While your attention was occupied trying to scare me a man came up in the lift, took one look at us and went down again. I strongly suspect he was Elroy Speke."

Jake swore and made a dash for the lift, but it wouldn't respond to his furious pressure on the button. "He must have jammed it open downstairs," Debbie observed. "It's too late now. Which means we've *both* managed to lose him today, and I'd say that left us about even. Wouldn't you, Inspector?"

The next day Debbie contacted Chief Superintendent Manners, her old mentor, and arranged to meet him for a drink after work. He choked with laughter at the story.

"All right, it wasn't that funny," she said crossly, watching his massive shoulders shake.

"It's hilarious," he said, wiping his eyes. "You and Jake Garfield, crossing each other's wires. I'll bet he was fit to die."

"Fit to kill, more like. Me."

"If you mucked up one of his cases I'm not surprised."

"He mucked up one of *mine*," Debbie said, seething.

"I'll bet that's not how he saw it."

"Oh, sure. He tried to make out it was all my fault. He's the rudest man I ever met."

"He doesn't like losing out."

"I asked you here because I wondered what you knew of him."

"I've worked with him a few times. I can't say I've taken to him. Few people do. He doesn't put himself out to be amiable. He does things his way and you like it or lump it."

"You used to bawl me out for doing much the same thing."

"True. But he does undercover work so he can get away with it more easily."

"Plus he's a *man* so he can get away with it more easily."

"Will you come off your soapbox?" Manners begged. "I've had a tough day."

"But it's true. You wouldn't have put *him* behind a desk."

"I wouldn't dare try. He's a very hard man. No vices, no weaknesses."

"Phooey!"

"Well, it's what they say. He became a bit of a legend. His nickname is Stoneface."

"That I can believe."

"Stone face, stone heart. That's the word on him. It's impossible to blackmail him, bribe him, flatter him or seduce him..." Manners looked at her curiously. "Unless you know differently?"

Debbie gave a reminiscent smile. "Well, I certainly ruffled his cool. Just how deep it went, I have yet to find out."

"I hope you haven't turned him into your enemy."

Debbie gave a choke of laughter. "I've turned him into a reluctant colleague. He wants me to help him snare Lucky Driver." She related the conversation and Manners whistled.

"I can see what he means, though," he said thoughtfully. "You could get under Lucky's skin if any woman could. Mind you, it's putting your head into the lion's den. It's not very gallant of him to shove you in there. Still, Stoneface never did think of anything but the job in hand."

"At least it shows he regards me as a serious colleague," Debbie observed.

"Yes..." Manners said slowly.

"Why do you say it like that?"

"Well, he doesn't like working with women. He says they're unreliable. I've heard him be downright insulting on the subject. You must have really impressed him."

"Oh, I impressed him all right," Debbie said. "As cannon fodder." She spoke crossly, for Jake's attitude was irritating. She was used to fending men off. What she wasn't used to was men who looked her beauty up and down and assessed its suitability for a job. His attitude was doubly insulting after what had passed between them in the hotel room. After that, he simply had no right to turn a cool, appraising eye on her. Still, she reflected, she had rather invited that approach.

To her surprise, three days passed before she heard from Jake. During that time the only thing that enlivened her boredom was a small newspaper item reporting that "entrepreneur Elroy Speke" had suffered a burglary at his office. It appeared that Mr. Speke had declined to call the police since he blamed himself for lax security, preferred not to cause trouble, and various other reasons all equally unconvincing. Nonetheless, the story had somehow found its way into the press, together with the information that every single paper in his filing cabinets had been removed, leaving only an empty shell and a note saying that the contents would be destroyed unread.

Debbie read this through carefully, then whistled in unwilling tribute to Jake Garfield.

The following evening she went out with a team she often worked with, trawling the city streets for homeless youngsters who could be taken to a safe place. With her huge, shapeless sweater, her face bare of makeup and her glorious fair hair pulled tightly back, she looked very different than the seductive beauty who'd attacked Jake's defenses so successfully a few days ago.

Coming home at two in the morning, she went into the darkened flat, and stopped, instantly alert. There was no sound or movement, but all her senses told her that she wasn't alone. She tensed, ready for action, but then some instinct made her say into the darkness, "I suppose the man who could burgle Elroy Speke so thoroughly would have no trouble with my locks."

"That's very good," said a cool voice.

She snapped on the light and saw Jake sprawled on her sofa. He had three days' growth of beard and looked as if he hadn't slept or eaten for at least that time. He rubbed his eyes as if it was an effort to keep them open. "I was expecting to hear from you before this," she said.

"My time's been rather taken up. A man I put away escaped from jail, hell-bent on killing me. He's back behind bars now, but I had to give him all my attention—well, almost all. Here." He handed her a large brown envelope.

Debbie pulled it open quickly. It contained the compromising pictures of Jane Quinlan, looking fifteen years younger than the woman Debbie knew. There was also a full set of negatives.

"I took everything he had and destroyed all the others," Jake said with a yawn. "But I thought you'd like to give these back to your client."

"She'll be thrilled," Debbie breathed. "Thank you." She colored suddenly. "I couldn't have done it so thoroughly."

"You underrate yourself. Your, er, talents would have achieved a result in the end."

"Yes, I could have gotten Jane's pictures, but I couldn't have saved all his other victims, the way you have," Debbie said honestly.

"You're a fair-minded woman," Jake said, regarding her. He sighed and added reluctantly, "I guess I can work with you."

"But you'd much rather not," Debbie said, goaded by his tone.

"But I'd much rather not," he agreed.

"You don't like working with women at all, do you?"

"Whatever gave you that idea?" he demanded sarcastically.

"Chief Manners. I asked him about you."

"What a coincidence. *I* asked him about *you*."

"According to him, you're known as Stoneface."

"He says you're brave, resourceful and trustworthy—"

"But?" For Jake's tone clearly contained a "but."

"But too prone to get some bee in your bonnet and forget everything else. In other words, you're unreliable, and to me that wipes out all the rest. And, yes, since you're asking, I'd say the same about any female colleague. I've worked with women before and always ended up swearing never, *never* again. I acted on impulse the other day and I wish I hadn't. Unfortunately it's too late to cancel the plan. My superiors are delighted with it, so I'm stuck with it."

"Stuck with *me,* you mean?"

"Yes," he snapped. "I must have been out of my head. You, of all people, with your scatterbrained way of working..."

"You can't forget one little mistake, can you?" she snapped.

"One little mistake was all right with me but it'll be one too many with Lucky Driver. He's a ruthless murderer. Do you know what happened to Liz James?"

"No."

"Neither do I, and that worries the hell out of me. She's vanished off the face of the earth. I hope that means she's gone into hiding but it might mean something more sinister."

"It makes it the right moment for me to appear in Lucky's life," Debbie said thoughtfully. "He's not only lost his woman, he's lost face. He needs a new woman on his arm, someone *spectacular.*"

The relish with which she said "spectacular" made Jake look at her sharply. For the first time he fully took in her shabby clothing and absence of makeup. It didn't matter, he realized. Her glorious sexual aura was so vital a part of her that it shone through her prosaic garments. It was there in her glowing skin, in the instinctive elegance of her movements. It breathed through her every pore. This was a woman whose sexuality could give a man heaven or hell. The hell he already knew about. The heaven was a dream whose fulfillment had been cruelly snatched away from him.

As he stared, the formless clothes seemed to become transparent, enabling him to see the beautiful frame beneath, as he'd seen it before, once in reality and every moment since in his unwilling consciousness. The memory dominated what little sleep he'd had these last few days.

"And you think you're spectacular enough for this assignment?" he asked ironically.

"Don't you?" she asked simply.

He took a deep breath. "I guess you already know the answer to that."

"I can be as spectacular as I have to be. Just leave the details to me."

He seemed to speak with an effort. "Well, now that we've got that settled, I can give you your orders."

Debbie stiffened at the word "orders." "How about we tackle this as a team of equals?" she said, trying to sound pleasant.

"No. How about we do it the efficient way, with me leading and you following?" he said curtly. "This is a police matter and the police must direct it."

It was a reasonable argument and if he'd spoken courteously Debbie would have accepted it, but his brusque tone set her back up. "So *you're* going to tell *me* how to win Lucky Driver's heart?" she challenged. "Perhaps you'd like to refer me to the appropriate chapter in the police manual."

He regarded her cynically. "I didn't think hearts were what you dealt in."

"I deal in whatever the job requires," she snapped.

"Yes, I remember. Now, can we talk practicalities? Driver is interviewing women for his floor show. You can meet him that way. The rest is up to you. But as soon as possible you get me a job close to him."

"Consider it done. Now I need some tea."

She went into the kitchen. When the tea was made she carried a cup out to him. But he made no response and she realized that he'd fallen asleep.

He lay with his head back against the cushions, his big body sprawled the length of the sofa. His clothes were shabby but they couldn't hide the magnificent lines of his frame. A frisson of remembered pleasure went through Debbie as she thought of how well she already knew that body, how she'd pressed it, almost naked, against her own, excited by the awareness of his strength. Now his limbs lay where they'd fallen, as though a puppet master had dropped the strings, yet the feeling of latent power was still there. Fate had made them antagonists, but the excitement wouldn't go away.

His hands lay still, as if they'd never been filled with tension, touching her urgently. They were shapely hands with long, blunt-ended fingers that spoke of skill and subtlety. She had to fight the temptation to touch them.

He looked exhausted. Beneath the dark stubble he was pale and drawn and there were shadows under his eyes. She considered his looks feature by feature. He was handsome but there was a lack of symmetry about his face that made it interesting. He had thick eyebrows that almost met over the top of his long nose. The angles of his jaw were sharply defined, and he had a stubborn chin.

She disliked him but she had to respect him. He'd dealt with Elroy Speke with a speed and thoroughness that was impressive. But it was his total absence of scruple that left her awed and secretly thrilled. She, too, had often ignored the book, but this man tore the book up and made a bonfire of the pieces, and there was a renegade streak in Debbie that responded to it with delight. In his uncompromising, quirky face, she saw the mark of the outsider that called to her. Crazy as it sounded, she and this man were fellow spirits.

He stirred, changing the angle of his head and giving her a better view. Sleep had smoothed away the harshness, which, she thought, improved him greatly. Now that his mouth was no longer issuing words of anger or sarcasm, she could see that the lower lip was curved and the shape of the whole had a surprising sensitivity. Somewhere inside that sensual body with its swiftly inflamed passions there was another man, with deep feelings. But he kept those feelings private, behind a door that was fiercely locked against the world. She leaned a little closer, enjoying her freedom to drink in everything about him.

And then he opened his eyes.

For a moment time stood still while they held each other's gaze. He didn't move, but lay there watching her with an intentness far back behind his eyes. His chest was rising and falling a little too fast for normal and Debbie could feel her own breath coming in quick gasps, matching him. She tried to move, but a hypnotic spell seemed to hold them both, while the moment stretched on and on. "Yes," he said at last. "It's going to be a problem, isn't it?"

Conventional words of disclaimer rose to her lips, only to die unspoken. To deny what they both knew to be the truth would be cowardly, and she was never that. "Only if we allow it to be," she said firmly.

"Allow?

"We're both mature adults, in control of ourselves."

"Are we?" His manner was grave but the wicked expression in his eyes was unsettling.

"Anybody can control themselves if they're sufficiently determined," she insisted.

Jake put a hand behind his head and surveyed her. "Is it going to be very hard to control yourself?" he asked with an air of innocence.

In the short pause that followed, Debbie contemplated murder. "No," she said curtly at last. "Actually it's going to be harder to force myself to work with you."

"That's how I feel, too," he said solemnly.

She took a deep breath. "I'd like to see you out of here."

His lips twitched. "I'd like to see you in bed."

"I beg your pardon!"

He unfurled himself from the sofa in one lanky movement, and went to the door. "Go to bed," he told her. "Get some sleep. You've an audition tomorrow, and you wouldn't like to blow this whole job by not getting hired, would you?"

"Do I tell you how to do your job?" she snapped, goaded beyond endurance.

He grinned. "Go to bed," he repeated, and vanished before she could react. His departure gave Debbie the chance to practice self-control. It took a lot of effort to suppress the desire to hurl a vase at the door, but she managed it.

Then she relaxed and an unwilling smile touched her mouth. There'd been something in his eyes that she hadn't expected from Stoneface, a hint of devilish humor behind the gravity. It had danced like a flame, and ignited another flame within her, disturbingly similar to the flames of their first meeting. On that day he'd brought her to life by his touch. Tonight there'd been no physical contact but she'd felt her flesh glowing again through the power of something that had exploded into life between them. Just what that something might be, she had yet to explore. It was made up partly of hostility, but a hostility rooted in the very opposite. Unwilling desire, attraction, fellow feeling. Out of these things had grown suspicion and rivalry. They were two people caught in an erotic spell that infuriated them, but which they couldn't deny.

"I think I'll do as he said and go to bed," she mused. "I'm going to need my sleep. Life has suddenly become very interesting."

Three

─────

From the outside, Lucky's Place practically didn't exist. There was a plain door in a wall in an elegantly luxurious part of London. Beside the door was a small brass plaque. That was all. The rich and famous, the notorious, the publicity seekers, the high-rolling gamblers, needed no more.

At night it was a place of discreetly dark corners interspersed with soft, colored lights. In the morning both the darkness and the soft lighting had gone, and the atmosphere was flat and chilly. Two men were sitting at a table near the stage, studying a line of young women who paraded slowly across. One of the men was squat and nondescript, and made busy notes the whole time. The other was in his mid-thirties and handsome in a fleshy way. He leaned back in his chair, right foot crossed over left knee, hands clasped behind his head, and regarded the procession with bored disdain. "Is this the best you can get, Des?" he demanded at last with a yawn.

Des, the squat one, who ran the nightclub on a day-to-day basis, grew aggrieved. "I think they're a pretty good bunch, Lucky."

"Pretty good? They look like showgirls."

"Well, they are showgirls."

"Then they're not good enough for me. The hostesses in this club must look like *ladies*. I had a cabinet minister in here last night. That's the kind of clientele I want, and you don't get it without class. Get rid of this crowd."

"You haven't seen them all yet—"

"I said, get rid of them. All right, girls, that's it."

"Not yet, it isn't."

Both men turned at the sound of a husky voice that came from just behind them. A tall woman wearing a long silk jacket and silver high-heeled sandals sauntered past and placed herself in front of them. "You haven't seen me yet, Mr. Driver," she said firmly, but in an enticing voice.

"Get lost!" Des ordered. "Auditions are closed for the day."

"Shut up, Des!" Lucky said, suddenly alert. His sharp eyes were fixed on the newcomer. "What's your name?"

The woman gently touched the very fair hair that swirled like a halo around her head and down onto her shoulders. "They call me Silver," she murmured. "And I'm a lady."

"You sure are," Lucky breathed. "And one hell of a woman. All right, let's see what you can do."

For answer Silver stepped onto the low cabaret stage and slipped off the jacket, revealing a perfect, long-limbed body attired in a minuscule white bikini. "I do this," she said simply, and had the satisfaction of seeing Lucky gulp.

She began to sing. It was a simple song with a narrow range that she could just encompass, but Lucky wasn't listening to the notes. He was hearing the promise in the throaty tone, and watching what she did with the silk jacket. In Debbie's hands the garment seemed to become something else. She twisted and turned, slithering it over her body so that she revealed tantalizing glimpses of herself and hid them again immediately. As the song ended she slipped the jacket on and buttoned it up to the throat, standing there, hands outstretched toward Lucky.

He sat motionless, his attention riveted on her. Debbie was reminded of a steer she'd once seen in a slaughterhouse. The beast had been humanely stunned first, and for a second had stood staring, poleaxed, before passing out. Now she saw the same blank, stupid expression on the face of the man she'd heard of as one of the most dangerous in London.

At last he seemed to recover his wits, and with them, his power of movement. He strode to a door at the side of the stage and looked back at her, snapping his fingers and jerking his head. "You—my office." When Debbie didn't move, he said impatiently, "Don't you hear me?"

"I hear you, Mr. Driver."

"Then what's keeping you?"

"I don't respond to having fingers snapped at me."

Lucky spoke with an edge on his voice. "Will you oblige me by coming to my office?"

"Certainly." Debbie sailed past him through the door.

His office was dark and masculine with oak paneling and a thick, velvety carpet. Debbie sat down in the chair he indicated. Lucky touched a switch that made a panel swing open, revealing a drinks cabinet. He poured two glasses of champagne and handed her one.

Debbie shook her head. "You didn't ask me what I wanted," she reproved. "I'll have mineral water, please."

Lucky made a wry face and poured her some mineral water. "A lady who knows her own mind. All right, but mineral water is poor stuff to celebrate the start of our association."

"I wonder if our association is going to be something I'll want to celebrate," Debbie said.

He perched on the edge of his desk and looked down at her. "It will be, Silver. You'll find that I treat my girls well."

"But I'm not a girl, Mr. Driver, and I don't like being called one."

A flash of temper hardened Lucky's brown eyes to stones. "And *I* don't like a woman who keeps putting me in my place. You're just an employee, don't forget that."

"But I'm not your employee, Mr. Driver, and I'm never going to be. You don't treat me with respect and I don't like that. So why don't we just stop wasting each other's time?"

Debbie rose to go. Quick as a flash Lucky put himself between her and the door. "Hey, don't be so touchy," he rallied. "I forgot my manners. I apologize."

She gave him the full blast of her most dazzling smile. "Your apology is accepted." She reseated herself, but when he held out the glass of mineral water, she shook her head. "I've changed my mind. I'll have champagne after all."

This time Lucky laughed. "You sure like to give a guy the runaround, don't you?"

"Most of them don't mind, actually."

"I'll bet they don't." He gave her champagne and she sipped it, looking at him over the rim, eyes twinkling.

She knew she presented a perfect picture, from her silvery fair hair to her long, silver-painted fingernails and silver toenails. Lucky seemed to think so, too, because he drew in a long, happy breath. "Tell me about yourself," he invited. "Have you done much of this kind of work before?"

"I've been around nightclubs a lot," Debbie said, going into a story she'd agreed on with Jake. "My husband owned one in Paris and I helped him run it."

"Husband?" Lucky's eyes dwelt on her bare left hand.

"My marriage is over," Debbie assured him. "I don't know where Jean-Pierre is now, except that he's on the run from the law somewhere." She allowed a brave, waiflike expression to flit across her face. "At one time I had a lot of money, but the crash left me without anything. Now I have to earn my living again."

The tale had been neatly crafted to suggest that she was used to existing on the wrong side of the law and asking no questions. Lucky studied her speculatively for a moment before refilling her glass. "What exactly did you used to do in this nightclub?" he asked.

"A little singing, a little dancing, but mostly I kept the customers happy. They knew I was the proprietor's wife and they appreciated that little extra attention." She looked deeply into Lucky's eyes. "I'm very good at the little extras, Mr. Driver."

"My name's Lucky," he said in a thick voice that sounded as if he were having trouble with his collar.

"Lucky by name and Lucky by nature?" she teased.

"Well, today is sure my lucky day."

Debbie looked at him enigmatically. "I hope you'll always think so," she murmured.

He grinned. "That's up to you, sweetheart. You treat me right and I'll treat you right. I've got big plans for you,

Silver. You're going to be a star. I'll spend a fortune making you look good.''

She shook her head. "I don't need your money to make me look good, Lucky," she said.

"Of course you don't. I just meant, nothing but the best for you. Here…'' He opened a wall safe and took out a box, which he thrust into her hand. "Open it,'' he said eagerly. Debbie did so and found a necklace of pearls. At a rough guess, she decided they would have paid her rent for a year.

She shrugged and handed them back to him.

"What's the idea?" he demanded, outraged.

"Pearls don't suit me. I'm more of a diamond sort of woman.''

"I'll buy you diamonds. I'll get you anything you want. But take these.''

"No, thank you. Put them away. You may need them for some other woman.''

"No other woman, sweetheart. From now on it's just you and me.''

He was looking like a poleaxed steer again, she noticed with interest. She was beginning to wonder about herself. Evidently her own powers were greater than she'd dreamed. Anyway, she was having fun.

"I'll have our lunch served here,'' he said.

She laughed. "I don't think so, Lucky. You're not a safe man for me to be alone with. But I'll allow you to take me to the Ritz.''

"The Ritz it is,'' he gabbled.

At the Ritz she feasted off caviar and champagne, and afterward Lucky drove her home in his Rolls-Royce. She allowed him to see her to the door but no farther. Lucky studied her cramped little hallway with disfavor. "I'm going to get you out of here into a decent place," he declared.

"Thank you, Lucky, darling," she cooed, "but I'm quite happy here."

"I don't want to visit you in a place like this."

"But you won't be visiting me," she assured him sweetly. "My home is my sanctuary, and I don't allow men inside."

Lucky scowled, but all he said was, "As long as you stick to that. No men in here. Ever."

She gave him a peck. "Who else could I ever want but you? Run along now. I need my afternoon nap."

He obeyed reluctantly. Debbie entered her flat and started the water in the shower. She'd just stepped out when there was a knock at her door. Wrapping the towel around her, she opened it cautiously and found a delivery boy with a package for her. Inside was a diamond bracelet that couldn't have cost less than five thousand pounds.

For perhaps the hundredth time Jake consulted his watch. The hands showed 3:30 a.m. and he was very weary of waiting, especially as the cramped little landing outside Debbie's flat offered nowhere to sit except the floor. It would have been easy to get inside as he'd done before, but it wouldn't have been wise. If Lucky returned home with her, and she invited him in, Jake would be discovered.

At last there was a noise from the street outside. He crept to the window, moving the curtain a crack. A Rolls-Royce had glided to a halt by the entrance to the apartment block. A man got out and held open a rear door, offering his hand at the same time. The woman who emerged was clad in a tight, black satin dress that showed off her curvaceous charms. Diamonds flashed in her ears, her elegantly coiffed hair and on her wrists.

As they came through the front door Jake positioned himself on the stairs that led up to the next apartment, ready to vanish from sight. He heard the woman say, "No, Lucky... you promised."

"C'mon, Silver, just for a few minutes."

"Not even for a few minutes. I told you that I don't allow men into my home."

"But that was before we got to know each other so well..." The man was pleading.

"Lucky, we don't know each other well. We don't know each other at all." Her voice had a throaty huskiness that made Jake's forehead start to sweat. He knew that note in her voice. It meant that this man was her prey, and she was leading him on, teasing him, making use of him.... And then, one day, the act would be over, the cat would pounce, showing her claws, revealing that it had all been a cruel game. Jake almost felt sorry for Lucky Driver.

There was the sound of a slight scuffle from below. "Just one more kiss, sweetheart," Lucky murmured.

"No. You don't know when to stop."

"After all the stuff I've given you why should I have to stop?" Lucky demanded. "Hey, what are you doing?"

"Returning your diamonds," the woman said in a suddenly firmer voice. "And you can have everything else you've given me."

"Hey, now, c'mon..."

"I never asked you for expensive gifts, Lucky. And you can have every last one back if you think they buy you any rights over me."

"Okay, okay, I didn't mean it. I'm sorry. I should have known better. Say you forgive me."

"Only if you're really sorry."

"I swear I'm sorry. It'll never happen again."

"Now be a good boy and run along."

After a moment there came the sound of the front door closing, then the rustle of satin as the woman walked up the stairs. She paused a moment, watching through the window as the Rolls glided away. Then she turned and gasped when she saw a man standing in the shadows just behind her. Instinctively she raised her hand to defend herself but he grabbed her wrist just in time. "It's only me," he said.

"So I see," she said crossly. "Don't take me by surprise like that. Another moment—"

"You'd have slugged me and and I'd have been lying unconscious at your feet," Jake finished ironically. "No way. This is one man who's never going to be at your feet."

"Suits me." Debbie opened the door to her apartment. "Come in," she said, "but stay by the door and don't put the light on."

He did so and watched as she drew the curtains across the windows, glancing down into the street again. "Is anyone there?" Jake asked.

"Not that I can see. But the other night Lucky stopped the Rolls around the corner and walked back to stand watching. I'm going to leave the main light out and put the kitchen light on." When she'd done so, she said, "Okay, it's safe for you to move now, but keep away from the window."

"How can you look him in the eye and swear no man has been in this apartment?" Jake mocked.

"No man has."

"Never?" he asked curiously.

"Never since I met Lucky."

"And before that?" He couldn't stop himself from asking.

Debbie folded her arms and looked at him with a teasing half smile that made him clench his hands out of sight. "Before doesn't concern you, Mr. Garfield."

Fool, he thought furiously, to expose himself to that one. "What about me?" he demanded. "I'm here."

She laughed. "You're a police officer. You don't count as a man." She put some coffee on, looking incongruous in her finery as she moved around the cramped kitchen. The black satin dress revealed the curves and hollows of her figure, clinging so tightly that Jake suddenly felt very hot. The swell of her hips and her long, beautiful flanks tormented him with their evocation of the day he'd seen her without clothes. Well, almost without clothes, he corrected himself reluctantly. She'd worn the wispiest bra and panties that had suggested as much as they'd concealed. But now the smooth line of the dress made it very obvious that she wore nothing underneath. Waves of heat surged through him and he resisted the temptation to run a hand around the inside of his collar. That would tell her everything, and he couldn't afford to give an inch with this woman. She was too confident of her power over men. Every glittering gem confirmed it.

"Are those real?" he asked, pointing to her wrist.

"I should damned well hope so. If he's a cheapskate who's been palming me off with fakes he'll hear about it."

"Aren't real diamonds a bit much to be asking for at this stage? You've only been with him a week."

"I'd only been with him a few hours when I got the first bracelet. I'm good at my job. You told me to get close to him and that's what I've done." Suddenly Debbie moved close and laughed directly up into Jake's face. "Lucky is just crazy about me," she murmured. "Couldn't you tell? I'm sure you were listening."

"Just checking how well you were doing. You've gotten it to a fine art, haven't you? Get the poor devil fretting his guts to fiddlesticks—allow him just so far and no further."

She regarded him mischievously. "I'm good at making men want me, Jake. You know that."

There it was between them, the memory of their desire, unwanted but unforgettable; the moments when they'd held each other, almost naked, burning up with a passion that had come sweeping out of nowhere to destroy their peace. They might try to put the thought aside but it was always there, threatening them, tormenting them, until it found some resolution. Looking into her eyes, Jake understood all this, and he came close to hating her for understanding it, too.

"You're so damned sure of yourself," he said bitterly, "but suppose when the moment comes you can't control him?"

She continued to stare at him, her lips twitching provocatively. "Not every man is a ravening beast, Jake," she said demurely. "Lucky is a gentleman."

"The hell he is! He's playing the game that suits him—"

"Well, I'm playing the game that suits me—and you."

"I repeat, suppose one night he won't be put off?"

"Then I'm sure you'll be lurking in the offing to, er, protect me."

She was laughing at him and there wasn't a damned thing he could do about it. "Why don't you change into something more prosaic?" he growled. "I'll see to the coffee."

Her lips moved silently, forming a word that might have been "coward," before she moved off to the bedroom. She closed the door and he saw the bar of light beneath it. By listening to the sounds he could tell exactly what she was doing. There was the slight clatter as she tossed her jewelry onto the dressing table, carelessly, as if a fortune in diamonds meant nothing to her; the click as she opened the wardrobe door, then a faint rustling that meant she'd let the dress fall to the floor. He pictured it sliding down her body, revealing her nakedness inch by inch. He tried not to but he couldn't help it. He was still fighting the inner battle when a scream from the coffee percolator brought him back to reality. He swore savagely as he mopped coffee from the stove.

"You're supposed to switch it off before it boils over," Debbie reproved. He glared at her, standing in the doorway, now wearing jeans and a shirt. "What on earth were you thinking of?"

"The case—anything—I don't know—" he said furiously.

Before she could speak there was a knock on the door. Debbie indicated with her head for Jake to vanish into her bedroom. "Who's there?" she called.

"Delivery for you, ma'am."

Debbie opened the door a crack and saw a man half hidden by a mountain of flowers. "Worldwide Flowers. Special delivery," he intoned from somewhere behind the blooms.

"Thank you. If you'll just wait a moment—"

"No tip necessary, ma'am. The gentleman gave me one and said I wasn't to take any money from you. Good night, ma'am."

Jake, listening at the door, heard the conversation clearly, followed by the sound of the door closing. While he waited for Debbie's signal to come out, he glanced around her bedroom, which he was seeing for the first time. He could have explored it the night he'd broken in to wait for her, but a sense of delicacy, which until that moment he hadn't known he possessed, had prevented him.

What he saw now was confusing. Her dressing table was plain to the point of austerity, with no sign of the creams and perfumes he would have expected. It might almost have belonged to a man. Even more forbidding was the rowing machine in the corner, which she obviously used to keep that glorious figure in perfect condition.

On the bedside table stood a large picture frame, turned to face the pillow so that the face it contained would be visible as soon as Debbie awoke. With a feeling of discovery he twisted it to him and read the words scrawled across the portrait. *My darling Max.*

Aha! Max!

But Max was a large Alsatian, his face split wide in a beaming grin.

"Thanks, Max," Jake murmured ironically.

The bed was the biggest puzzle of all: too large for one, too small for two, unless those two were very close. Like everything else in the room it was functional. There were no scatter pillows or mascots propped against the head. The bedside table contained a lamp, a telephone and a book called *Advanced Steps In Martial Arts*. Apart from Max there was no photograph to suggest that anyone held a special place in her life. Jake thought of the way he'd first seen her, removing her clothes with deliberate seductiveness, then tonight as Silver, an exotic, perfumed creature, designed to lead a man to perdition.

As he'd told Debbie, Jake had checked up on her with Chief Manners. But what he hadn't told her was that he'd done some further checking among her lowlier colleagues, and the results had interested him more than he cared to admit. Detective Sergeant Harker had a reputation as a heartbreaker, who could have any man she pleased, and knew it. Men had spoken of her in the wistful tones of those who yearned without reward. She'd evidently given her favors very sparingly, if at all, and the impression grew on him of a woman with supreme confidence. No, not confidence, he amended, remembering how she'd stripped in the hotel room. Arrogance. It had called to an arrogance of his own, challenging it like fire, and arousing a reaction in which admiration and antagonism were about evenly mixed.

But there was no trace of that side of her in this nunlike room. Jake stood looking around him, baffled.

"Okay, you can come out now," Debbie called, pushing the door open. He went out to find that she'd switched on a small reading lamp. By its light he could see not merely the huge bouquet that had just been delivered but, also, the rest of the apartment, which was almost buried under flowers. "Good grief!" he exclaimed. "White roses. The place is covered in them."

"I get a delivery every day," Debbie said. "This is an extra one." She studied the card that had come with the bouquet, a little smile touching her lips. "Lucky's outdone himself."

Jake took the card from her and read it.

My lady's smiles are all my life.
My lady's frowns do end my life.
Forgive me, sweetheart.

Lucky

"Ye gods!" Jake exclaimed in disgust. "Does he write that kind of stuff himself?"

"It sounds like him. He has pretensions to being a poet. Lucky doesn't understand poetry but he thinks it's classy. Like me."

"You mean he thinks *you're* classy?" Jake echoed, eyeing her with misgiving.

"Of course," Debbie said airily. "I keep him at arm's length. I take from him but give nothing back except a tiny peck. I set a very high price on myself, and to a man who puts a price on everything there's nothing classier than that."

"You think you've got him taped, don't you?"

"Mostly. I know he enjoys being kept dangling. Lucky's a romantic. He likes to put his lady on a pedestal."

"Smiling and frowning on him?" Jake said with the plain man's disgust at flowery sentiment. "What a load of rubbish!"

"Your trouble is that you can't appreciate the lofty sentiments that unite Lucky and me," Debbie told him severely. "We're soul mates. In each other's company we think only beautiful thoughts."

"What *he* thinks about is undressing you."

"Well, isn't that a beautiful thought?" she asked demurely.

Caught off guard, Jake threw down the card he'd been holding and snapped, "If he's so crazy about you, how come he isn't sending you *red* roses yet? Aren't they the flowers of love?"

"Fancy you knowing that!" she said scathingly.

"I may not be a sensitive soul who writes poetry," Jake growled, "but I know a few things about men and women, and if he's that mad about you they should be red."

Debbie regarded him pityingly. "He sent me red roses on the first day, and I sent them back," she explained. "I told him white were the only kind I'd accept. He likes that. Pure and untouchable, that's me."

"Oh, really! He should have seen you as I've seen you."

Debbie chuckled. "He did. Just once, for a few minutes at the audition. Since then he's been tying himself in knots trying to see it again."

Jake, who knew the feeling, regarded her with dislike.

"Poor Lucky," Debbie mused softly, and to Jake's lacerated sensibilities it sounded like "Poor Jake."

"When are you going to get me inside his organization?" he asked sharply.

"As a matter of fact I was going to call you tonight. Two of Lucky's henchmen have 'disappeared.' He was mad at them for some slipup, and since then neither of them has been seen again."

"Which means they're probably at the bottom of the river," Jake mused.

"Probably. Somebody came for a job today, but didn't get it. I thought he was a sure thing but then Brian jumped him. Brian is Lucky's right hand—nasty looking brute with a squashed nose. He just attacked this man without warning and knocked him out. Lucky looked down at him and said, 'If he was of any use he couldn't have been surprised so easily. Get him out of here.' So if you're coming to see Lucky, watch out for Brian."

"Thanks for the warning," Jake said ironically. "I'd never have thought of that for myself."

"I believe you."

"Don't push your luck, Miss Harker."

"I push my luck every day I go into the lion's den," she reminded him. "If I'm not afraid of Lucky, why should I be afraid of you?"

"If you had any sense you *would* be afraid."

"Of him—or of you?"

He regarded her. "What do you think?"

"I have the strangest feeling that you'd like me to be afraid of you. But you're not going to succeed, and I think you already know that."

He took a deep breath. "I haven't time to stand here talking nonsense. Is there a rear exit to this block, just in case he's still about?"

She accompanied him to the rear exit and locked it behind him. As she returned to her flat she mused on the way that she was fighting on two fronts. There was the struggle with Lucky, and there was the more difficult battle with the rude, ill-tempered man who'd mysteriously gotten under her skin. Jake wouldn't yield an inch, yet he stirred her blood in a way that Lucky's slavish devotion never could. Now she had to make him admit that he wanted her without letting him suspect how desperately she wanted him. That was all.

Jake presented himself at Lucky's about six hours later. He reckoned it would make a good impression to turn up early. If it had crossed his mind that Debbie was unlikely to be about so soon he would have suppressed the thought as unprofessional. Just the same, he wasn't sorry to avoid having her mocking eyes on him as he approached Lucky.

To get that far he had to first be looked over by a man who didn't give his name but whom Jake guessed must be Brian. His squashed nose fitted Debbie's description. So did his general air of unpleasantness. He asked a few questions that Jake answered in monosyllables designed to give the impression that he was a petty crook. At last Brian took him over to where Lucky sat at a table in the corner of the club, studying figures. "There's a bloke here reckons he wants a job, boss," Brian said.

Lucky looked up. Even at this hour of the morning he was immaculately dressed, with every hair in place and his nails perfectly manicured. A surge of dislike went through Jake, startling him with its suddenness and ferocity.

"What's your name?" Lucky asked.

"Jake Blair."

"So you want a job? Why here? Why now?"

"Heard you might have something."

Lucky's eyes narrowed. "How did you hear that?"

Jake's manner became shifty. "I was in this place—lots of us there—left yesterday morning." Lucky nodded, evidently understanding this roundabout way of referring to prison. "I went to a hostel," Jake went on, "and the word's out that two of your blokes left suddenly." Lucky stirred and Jake tapped the side of his nose. "No questions," he said with a wink. "But I heard someone tried yesterday and didn't suit."

Lucky nodded. "Know why he didn't suit?"

"Not exactly."

"He wasn't man enough for the job. Think you are?"

Mindful of Debbie's warning, Jake had placed himself where he could see Brian out of the corner of his eye. Even so, he was only just in time. As the thug leapt on him Jake sidestepped swiftly and felled him to the ground. Brian clutched his nose, which was bleeding from the blow.

"Sorry," Jake said laconically. "Pity to spoil a nice nose like that."

Pure hate gleamed in Brian's eyes as he hurled himself forward. This time Jake finished the job with one blow that left Brian crumpled in a corner. "Anything else you want done?" he asked of Lucky.

Lucky grinned. "Not bad," he murmured. "Not bad at all." He used the toe of his shoe to nudge Brian, who was opening his eyes and shaking his head. "Get up," he said in disgust. "And clear out of my sight." Brian flung Jake a look that boded ill and moved off.

"You could be useful to me," Lucky told Jake. "What else can you do? Drive?"

"There are men who owe their freedom to my driving," Jake said.

"Good, good. All right, I'll take you on. You'll be a gofer at first, make yourself useful in any way I want. If I'm satisfied, the sky could be the limit." He stood back and regarded Jake. "If you only got out yesterday you probably need some money."

"I'm a bit short," Jake agreed.

Lucky tossed a wad of bills at him. "Make yourself presentable. You'll be driving a lady." His face lit up at something he'd seen over Jake's shoulder. "Silver, sweetheart, there you are."

He took Debbie into his arms. Jake looked at her over his shoulder. Every line in his body spoke of boredom and indifference, but actually he was acutely aware of her running a hand up Lucky's arm to his shoulder and letting her fingers trail playfully over his face. Jake gritted his teeth and forced himself to look away. Some devil had taught her that those light, frisky touches were the most difficult to withstand. *Jezebel.*

As Debbie and Lucky moved off, he heard her voice, full of rippling laughter, ask, "Who on earth is that?" He couldn't make out Lucky's answer, but her next words drifted back to him. "Looks like something the cat brought in."

Four

Next morning Jake was formally introduced to "Silver." Lucky summoned him to the office and there he found Debbie leaning against the wall, delicately sipping champagne.

"Silver, sweetheart, this is Jake, my new man. He's going to drive you into town."

Silver looked the new man over indifferently and gave the faintest nod of her head in response to his polite greeting.

"And this is for you," Lucky said, producing a gold credit card. "Get yourself any little thing you want. 'Bye now." He leaned down to kiss her lightly, but Silver wrapped an arm about his neck and drew him close. Jake gritted his teeth and looked out the window.

"Hey," Lucky said after a while, "I'll have to send you shopping more often if I get this response."

"I just like showing my gratitude," Silver told him in a husky voice. She sauntered to the door. "'Bye, darling. Think of me while I'm away."

Jake kept his face expressionless while he followed her downstairs and out to the car. As soon as the doors were closed on them Debbie looked at him, her eyes twinkling, but the laughter died when she saw him frowning and shaking his head.

"What . . ." She fell silent as she saw the finger over his lips. Then he directed his hand beneath the dashboard. She could see something small and hard. Her jaw fell open as she realized that this was a bug. Plainly, Lucky didn't trust anybody.

"Where are we going, ma'am?" Jake asked formally as he started the car.

Debbie assumed a distant voice. "I need a fitting for my costume in the floor show." She gave him the address.

When they reached the theatrical costumer's, he said, "Do you want me to wait out here?"

"Of course not," she informed him loftily. "You can carry my purse."

Jake closed the car door a little harder than necessary and walked beside her. Now that they were well away from the bug he ventured to whisper furiously, "You're loving this, aren't you?"

She smiled. "I get so few pleasures in my simple life."

"What are you doing in the show, anyway?"

"I'm the star. Lucky's building the whole thing around me."

"Is that wise?" he asked ironically.

She refused to be provoked. "Lucky thinks it is. He thinks I'm the greatest thing since sliced bread. Actually, I can sing reasonably. I don't need a very big voice in that place."

In the costumer's he was forced to wait, looking and feeling horribly out of place, while Debbie went into a cubbyhole. At last she emerged and glided across the room before him, regarding herself in floor-length mirrors. Jake surveyed her, trying not to let his jaw drop.

The dress was skintight and made of what appeared to be pure silver glitter. Whenever she moved, it flashed blindingly. Her waist seemed impossibly tiny and above it her breasts were full and womanly. But what outraged Jake was that the cleavage came right down to the waist, front and back. Worse, the skirt of the dress was slit right up the side as far as her waist. Everything was designed to provoke the onlooker to wonder what, if anything, she was wearing underneath. And to draw his own conclusions.

"Do you think it's effective?" Debbie asked. Receiving no reply, she turned to see Jake breathing hard. "Well?"

"It's effective," he growled. "I'll admit that."

"Good. That's all that matters, after all." She turned to the assistant. "Fine. I'll take it."

When they'd locked the dress into the car he escorted her around the shops. "It's safe to talk, isn't it?" she asked when his silence became noticeable.

"I'm trying to think of the right words."

"About what?"

Unable, or unwilling, to express his own feelings, he resorted to projecting them onto his employer. "I think you've made a fundamental miscalculation," he informed her coldly. "Lucky won't like you flaunting your body in that thing."

"You're an expert, are you?"

Just in time he saw the trap and avoided it. "No man who was crazy about a woman could stand her exhibiting herself in front of other men like that," he said stiffly.

"Really? Tell me about it, Jake." Her eyes teased him with their shared knowledge.

"I know more about male psychology than you do," he snapped, "and I'm telling you—"

"But you don't know about Lucky's psychology. That's a stage dress, only to be worn when there's a safe distance between me and the spectators. He just loves other men to admire me—"

"They're not going to admire you, they're going to drool over you."

"Well, he loves that, too, as long as everyone knows I'm strictly his."

"I still say you've got it wrong. He'll go mad when he sees that thing."

"You're the one who's got it wrong. Lucky's already seen the design and loved it. So I'm doing my job properly and I don't know what you're making a fuss about."

Jake threw her a sulphurous glare. "Are we going to be in this shop much longer?" he demanded. "I don't know why they don't get some air-conditioning. The place is like an oven."

Her lips twitched. "Getting hot under the collar, Jake?" she asked sweetly.

He took a deep breath. "One day, Miss Harker, this is going to be over, and then—"

"And then we'll go our separate ways, and never meet again. Isn't that so?"

"You know better than that," he said in a low voice. "Going our separate ways is not what the stars have lined up for us."

"The stars? Fancy you believing in astrology!"

"I didn't mean—"

"Imagine, Stoneface being superstitious! Suppose that got around the force?"

"Just let this job be over quickly," Jake implored an unseen deity through gritted teeth. "That's all I ask."

They spoke little on the journey home. Jake asked if she was comfortable and she replied distantly that she was. At one point she said, "I believe Mr. Driver gave you some money to smarten yourself up?"

"Yes, ma'am."

"Then do it, and quickly. I'm choosy who I'm seen with."

"Yes, ma'am."

Lucky, listening to this conversation relayed to his office via the bug, smiled in satisfaction. There was no doubting it. That Silver was a real lady.

Debbie put the last touch of makeup in place and studied her mirror image critically. She was about to make her first appearance as the star of the floor show, and on the whole she was pleased with the effect. Her hair had been piled high on her head, save for a few curved strands that whispered about her neck. Every feature of her face had been heightened for effect, and there was no trace of her true self in the superglamorous creature who gazed back at her. She was Silver, queen of Lucky's Place, and also of Lucky's heart.

Harry, the musical arranger and conductor, had made a careful choice of songs, and even written one specially for her limited range. As a dancer she was reasonably good, having danced as a hobby most of her life and even experimenting with a brief career as a hoofer. But her modest talents caused her no fears. Her chief job, as she knew, would be to stand there looking gorgeous and making every man in the place envy Lucky.

"Oh, Mom!" she murmured. "If you could only see me now!" Then she gave a little self-deprecating smile and added, "You'd say your worst fears had been exceeded. You always predicted I'd come to a bad end, but even you never saw me as a gangster's moll."

She thought of her sedate, kindly parents, and how baffled they'd always been by her. Her father was a university professor, her mother a teacher, and to them only the life of the mind really counted. But life presented itself to Debbie through her instincts, especially her physical ones. Color, sound, touch: the impressions poured in through her senses, making all of life brilliant. Even now her gut reaction to a person was what counted. Her head would think up reasons later. Her achievements had always come by following her instincts. Her problems had come by ignoring them. Her gut reaction to Jake had been "Wow!" His touch had brought her flesh to life as no other man's had done, and she couldn't hide from herself that she longed to feel it again.

Since that first day they'd been careful never to touch each other, even by chance. They were like joint guardians of a precious object, circling the treasure, eyeing each other warily, silently challenging each other to make the first move, knowing that an instant's clumsiness could cause fatal damage.

The battle between them was no less intense for being unacknowledged. Each of them would gladly go to the stake before being the first to admit weakness. Jake had achieved the first hit the night he'd broken into her flat, when he'd asked if it would be hard for her to control herself. No, she amended, that was his second hit. His first had been his willingness to throw her into the lion's den for the sake of the job. She was perfectly willing to go in among the lions, but Jake's matter-of-fact use of her didn't look like a man in the grip of uncontrollable passion.

But she'd evened the score at the dress fitting. The costume had shredded his control almost into tatters, she reflected with satisfaction.

Lucky was sleek, handsome, lavishly generous, and her worshipful slave, but he left her cold. It wasn't just the knowledge that behind the ardent exterior he was a ruthless criminal. Even without that there would be something missing for a woman whose senses obstinately persisted in responding to a harsh, irritable man who'd threatened her with arrest and then blackmailed her into danger.

Lucky came in, bringing with him the reek of costly after-shave. He wore a dinner jacket and bow tie, and diamond studs gleamed on his cuffs. "There's a big crowd out there tonight, sweetie," he said. "Nervous?"

The truthful answer would have been, "Not a bit," but Debbie knew better than to say that. She favored Lucky with a dazzling smile and cooed, "The only thing I'm nervous about is the thought of letting you down."

"That could never happen," he responded gallantly. "Here." He offered her a flat, black box. Inside were diamond pendant earrings gleaming against black velvet.

"Oh, Lucky!" she said breathlessly. "You spoil me!"

"It's no more than you deserve, sweetheart," he said, fastening them on. "Of course, any time you feel like thanking me properly—but I'm not rushing you," he added hurriedly. "Don't think that. Everything will be just as you like."

She ran a hand down his face. "Be a little more patient. I have to be on stage in a moment. But you're so sweet."

She let him kiss her. It was like being kissed by a dead haddock.

A few moments later she was waiting behind the glittering curtain while the master of ceremonies announced, "And now, our special guest star, straight from Paris, all for your delight, the delectable—Silver!"

The band struck up. Debbie stepped into the spotlight to a storm of applause. She wasn't deceived by it. She knew, because Jake had told her, that all Lucky's employees had been ordered to cheer and clap on pain of the direst penalty.

"So you cheer louder than anyone," she'd commanded him. "That's the least I expect."

"Yes, ma'am," he'd replied ironically.

The spotlight dazzled her but she still managed to discern Jake, leaning against the wall watching her intently. When the applause died and she began to sing, it was Jake who held her attention by his total stillness. All she could see was his outline, but she knew he was following her tiniest movement, listening to her slightest inflection.

"You're the one for me...." she crooned. "Only you—only you."

Her eyes, full of a knowing twinkle, flickered across the front row. A sigh went up from the men assembled there, and their womenfolk looked at them sharply.

"At night, when I'm alone in my bed, I think of you—only you."

A less shrewd woman would have concentrated on the word "bed." Debbie chose "alone," singing it with a sighing emphasis that made every red-blooded man in the place think of precisely the opposite. She smiled in complicity, letting them all know she understood their torment. Letting one man know.

"You're in my thoughts every moment—only you."

Her voice whispered huskily into the silence. She bowed her head as the lights came up to the sound of applause. After a moment she raised her eyes, but Jake was gone.

Lucky led the applause ecstatically, then escorted Debbie to the table where he was sitting with a group of men. They all paid her admiring compliments and she responded with an inane smile, while mentally noting their names.

She stayed with them for an hour, observing which ones Lucky seemed to consider important and giving them her special attention. Lucky was bursting with pride, until the moment one of them put an arm about Debbie's waist and tried to draw her close. Then the geniality died out of his expression and he freed her with firm hands. "Don't get carried away, Arthur," he said. "Remember whose she is." His lips were still stretched in a smile but his eyes were cold.

"I think I'll go home now," Debbie murmured.

Lucky took her out into the corridor, his arm about her. "You did great tonight," he said. "Don't worry about that punk. He won't bother you again. I've got to get back to them. Jake will take you home."

Jake was waiting for her when she reappeared a few minutes later in outdoor clothes. Silently she handed him a sheet of paper on which she'd written the names of the men she'd met tonight, and various small scraps of information she'd gleaned from the conversation. He nodded and pocketed the paper.

When they reached her apartment block he stopped and got out. They faced each other in the street. By the light

of a street lamp she could see the strain on his face.
"Good night," he said politely.

"Aren't you going to see me to my door, Jake?"

"I think I'll stay here."

"But you're supposed to be ensuring my safety."

His iron control snapped. "Damn it, I *am* ensuring
your safety," he said raggedly.

"By keeping your distance?"

"*Yes.*"

She smiled in triumph. "Well, that's nice to know.
Night, Jake."

It was two weeks after Silver's triumphant opening at
Lucky's Place that George opened the door of his seedy
little studio and found his worst fears realized. "Now,
look, I was only doing my job," he said in a placating
voice. "Just a hired hand, that's all."

"You'll be just a lump of squashed jelly if you give me
any trouble," Jake said grimly. "Get inside."

George backed into the studio, followed by Jake. An
unclad female sitting in a provocative posture on a plinth
stared at them. "The session's over for today," Jake informed her. "Get dressed and go."

"What about my fee?" she demanded.

Jake stuffed some money into her hand. She regarded
the amount wide-eyed, then scuttled away before he could
change his mind. "Er... I haven't finished with her yet,"
George protested.

"Yes, you have, George," Jake informed him, still in
the same deadly pleasant voice that filled the photographer with apprehension. "You have no further business
today—except with me." He waited until the studio door
had closed behind the model before demanding, "Where
are they? And don't waste my time asking what I mean

because you know damned well. You also know what I am, don't you? I expect Miss Harker called and told you.''

"Well, yes," George admitted reluctantly. "She did say you were filth, er, pig—er, police." He wiped his brow, wishing he were dead.

"Right the third time," Jake agreed. "So I want those pictures and negatives."

George's courage revived enough for him to assume a shocked expression. "You don't think I've still got them, do you? As soon as I knew you were fil—police, I did my civic duty and destroyed the lot."

Jake didn't even bother to answer this. He merely treated George to a smile that made him turn pale and start rummaging frantically. At last he produced a brown envelope and held it out to Jake, who took it. "Nice," he observed, running through the pictures. "All the negatives here? No, a couple missing I fancy."

"How would you know?" George was indignant enough to forget his nervousness.

"Well, I recall everything that happened and I imagine that you snapped it all. So—there are some missing. You can either give them to me or I can search for them. I expect your files would make a very interesting investigation, George. I don't suppose Speke was the only one."

"Now there you're wrong," George said insistently. "Straightforward titillation, that's my line. I never went in for anything dubious before."

"Nothing but clean, honest pornography until ex-Detective Sergeant Harker corrupted you?" Jake said with a grin. "All right, I'll believe you. Just give me the missing negs."

Sighing, George did so. Jake glanced at them, grunted and put them away. "One last thing," he said. "It's taken me several weeks to track you down. You could have done a lot in that time, so I want to know. Just who else has received a copy of these?''

"No one," George yelped.

"What about Miss Harker? Surely she wanted a copy?"

"No, she just said don't let them fall into the wrong hands."

"Come on, how many did you give her?"

"None, I swear it. She didn't want any. When she knew you weren't Speke she said the pics weren't of any interest."

Jake stared at him for a moment. "All right. But watch your step, George, because if any of those pics turn up on the market your life is going to become very, very difficult. Understood?"

George gulped. "Understood."

Jake walked out of the studio without a backward glance, feeling as if the photographs were burning him. He'd have liked to study them as soon as he was in the car, but he guessed George was watching from the window above, so he resisted temptation. As he drove he reflected on George's last words. "When she knew you weren't Speke she said the pics weren't of any interest." For some reason that had annoyed him. But, after all, what the hell did he care whether she found him of interest or not?

When the car was out of sight George dropped the curtain, went hurriedly to the phone and dialed Debbie's number. As he'd feared, she was out and he was forced to talk to her answering machine.

"He found me," he said. "I had to give him the pics. He wanted to know if you'd had copies and I swore blind that you hadn't. So for Pete's sake, don't let him find that set of enlargements you insisted on having, or I'm for the high jump. 'Bye."

* * *

When Debbie arrived at the club in the early evening Lucky was usually there to greet her. On this occasion there was no sign of him and she headed for his office. But when she reached the corridor she stopped. She could hear Lucky's voice from behind the door, and he was clearly in a rage. "Tell him if he screws me around he'll be sorry," he shouted. "A deal's a deal."

Debbie moved slowly closer, her feet noiseless on the thick carpet.

"I don't give a damn what he thinks!" Lucky screamed. "The stuff'll be there tomorrow and the money had better be there, too." There was a loud noise as though Lucky had slammed down a telephone.

Debbie took a deep breath and walked in, all smiles. "I missed you, lover," she told him. "Where's my first kiss of the evening?"

He kissed her but for once it was an absentminded gesture and he immediately turned away and began to pace his office, muttering as he went. "Okay, so I was late by one day. One lousy, stinking day! So what? The money that jerk's made outta me... He knows I've been having problems."

"Who, darling?"

"That damned Greek!" Lucky snapped. "You know what he dared to do? Sent me a message by some little punk to say he was deducting twenty percent from the money. Twenty percent. *One lousy day!*" His voice rose into an almost demented shriek. Debbie stared at him, startled by the suddenness with which his smooth facade had crumbled. Then her excitement began to grow as she realized she'd been given an unexpected chance.

"Well, maybe that day was important to him," she said casually.

Lucky swung around and looked at her with sheer, cold malevolence. "Are you taking his side against me?" he demanded. *"Is that what you're doing?"*

Debbie thought fast. The last thing she wanted was Lucky getting suspicious of her, even if his suspicions pointed the wrong way. She gave a sudden wail and collapsed onto the sofa, sobbing violently.

"Hey, hey—come on," Lucky said hastily. "I didn't mean—don't cry, sweetheart—"

"I don't know what I've done to make you mad," she wept. "I don't understand anything—"

"Of course not. When I lose my temper I don't know what I'm saying." He sat beside her and took her into his arms. "I'm a clumsy idiot," he castigated himself.

Debbie sobbed louder. "How could I be on the Greek's side against you, Lucky? I don't even know who he is."

"Sure you don't. Let's just keep it that way."

She wiped her eyes and sniffed bravely. "Perhaps you should tell me about him. Then I'll know how to avoid him."

"He's just a guy I do business with..."

"You mean, like those men who come every night? I thought we were going to have supper together last night and then they came and you just sent me home and—"

"Hell, sweetheart, I have to do business. Where do you think I get the money to pay for your little trinkets? Here..." He rummaged in his desk and brought out a wad of notes that he stuffed into her hand. "Buy yourself something pretty."

She kissed him and left the office, feeling that she'd done a good day's work. She was curious about the strange visitors who'd started to call after hours. Whenever possible Lucky liked to drive Debbie home himself, but, as she'd complained to him, his visitors took priority. On those occasions he delegated the job of chauffeuring Debbie to Jake. On the journey Jake would switch on the radio and they would say little, mindful of the bug under the dashboard.

He'd never again refused to come inside the flat with her. After that one night his cool mask was in place again, which Debbie found annoying. When they reached her home he would come inside, but only for a brief discussion. "Who are these men?" he asked her that night when they reached her door.

"I don't know, but they're important. They gather in his office."

"Do you meet them?"

"Usually. Lucky likes to introduce me so that he can show me off. They're very guarded while I'm there, but I do know that they're planning something big. Lucky talks to different people every night, but soon he's going to get them all together. And I overheard him on the phone this afternoon." She related everything that had happened. "Unfortunately he calmed down too soon, or I'd have learned more. When he loses his temper he talks too much."

"Be careful you don't push him over the edge," Jake said dryly.

"Don't worry about me."

"I'm not," he said untruthfully. "I'm worried about the job."

"Well, don't be. I'm getting you the information and I'll go on getting it. Lucky *adores* me."

"He needs his head examined."

She leaned back against the doorjamb and looked at him provocatively. "Don't you understand how he feels, just one tiny little bit?"

"Not a bit. You're more trouble than you're worth,"
he growled.

Debbie gave a deep, husky laugh that shredded him into
little pieces. "That's what Lucky says, too," she told him.
"But he always gives me a present straight afterward to
show what he really thinks of me."

Jake's eyes glinted. "Shall I show you what I really
think of you?" he demanded.

"Would I like it?"

"Suppose we try?" He was leaning toward her as he
spoke. Her lips were beginning to part, he could feel her
sweet breath as she parted them wider....

Then she yawned, covering her mouth with her hand
and making a theatrical performance of it. "D'you know,
I'm suddenly very tired," she declared. "It came over me
without warning."

He stepped back as though scalded. Fooled again!
"How I keep my hands off you I don't know," he said
grimly.

She looked at him impishly. "Well, if you don't know,
I certainly don't." She slipped inside before he could reply, and he found himself facing a closed door.

Five

"Jake, in my office a moment."

Jake followed Lucky into the office and waited while he closed the door. "I have to be away on urgent business for a few days," Lucky explained. "Now, I trust you, so I'm going to put something really important in your hands."

Jake's heart began to beat with excitement. This was it, the chance to get into the thick of it that he'd been waiting for. He came out of his happy dream to realize that Lucky was still talking. "So it's best if Brian comes with me and you stay here."

Jake's head jerked up. "You're going to take that gorilla and not me?" he exclaimed in disgust.

Lucky grinned. "I agree he's a gorilla, but my friends know him. They're nervous people. They don't like having strangers sprung on them."

"So take both of us. Then your friends can get used to me."

"Who'd look after Silver? She has to be protected." He put a hand on Jake's shoulder. "I'm putting my most precious treasure in your hands."

With difficulty Jake restrained himself from snorting. To be cut out of the action to watch over that maddening woman who needed protecting about as much as Attila the Hun needed it! That was gall and wormwood.

"By the way," Lucky added, "she called to say she wants you to collect her for some shopping. Better get going."

Debbie's shopping turned out to be a gold signet ring with the words Remember Me While You're Away, Silver. engraved inside. Jake's eyes opened wide at the price, and even wider when he saw Debbie pay in cash. "Where the hell did you get that much?" he demanded as they left the shop. "From Lucky, of course. He gave it to me yesterday, to make up for being mean to me. I thought it was time I gave him something to prove my devotion. Do you think he'll like it?"

"He'll be thrilled. Where you're concerned he's a big enough fool for anything."

"How ungracious!" she teased, and broke into a laugh at the scowl he flung her.

Lucky was more than thrilled. He was like a child receiving the first present at Christmas. "Gee, sweetheart, no one's ever given me anything like this before. Most women just take, but you're different. Hey, Blair, look at this! Isn't she some classy lady?"

Jake had a disconcerting desire to yell, "Wake up to her! You know damned well she bought it with your own money. She's making a fool of you and you love it. Have some dignity, man!"

But he gritted his teeth and watched in silence as Lucky produced his own parting gift, a necklace of sapphires and diamonds, and draped it around Debbie's neck. She wore it onstage that night and sang the torch songs with significant glances toward Lucky. In the middle of the last song he blew her a kiss and departed.

Half an hour later Jake knocked on Debbie's dressing room door and heard her call out, "Come in."

He entered to find that she'd just finished changing. The sequined creation had been replaced by jeans and sweater and her hair hung free without its decoration of gems. The heavy makeup had also been scrubbed off, leaving only her natural beauty. "Are you ready to go home, ma'am?"

"Quite ready, thank you, Blair. You can take my bag."

"Yes, ma'am."

In the street outside she surveyed the car he'd brought around for her. "What's this?"

"Mr. Driver has taken the Rolls with him, ma'am. I said I'd use my own car." He opened the door for her.

"But this isn't your car," she said as he got in. "It's a station wagon. You wouldn't be seen dead in it normally."

"It belongs to a colleague on the force. I borrowed it because my own car didn't fit my image as Lucky's errand boy— since that's all I seem to be," he finished angrily.

"Is Lucky annoyed with you?" she asked as he started up the engine.

"Far from it. He's so pleased with me that he's put his most precious treasure into my care. In other words, you." The bitterness in his voice made Debbie smile to herself. If she'd wanted to get Jake's goat, she could congratulate herself on having got it.

When they'd made half the journey in silence she said, "You really are mad at me, aren't you?"

"It would have been more helpful if Driver had taken me with him."

"And I'm to blame for that?"

Of course she was to blame, he thought savagely. She was to blame for being so seductive that she dominated a man's thoughts and senses, so that even when he wasn't with her she was always there, just around the corner of his mind, the craving for her coloring every other experience. She was to blame for being so enchanting that— Hell, no! Not enchanting. What was he thinking of? Enchanting implied another world beyond the sensual, like when her eyes held delicious laughter that caused a wellspring of delight to leap up inside him, even when her mockery was directed at himself. Enchantment was for the Lucky Drivers of the world, who didn't know it was all an act. You couldn't succumb to magic when you knew how the trick was worked.

"Well?" she asked. "Have you found a way of blaming me? If you haven't, I'm sure it's not for want of trying."

"Quiet. I'm concentrating on the road."

"Strange, I'd have thought you could do that and talk as well," she said sweetly. "But I suppose some men are more limited than others."

He ground his teeth. Definitely not enchanting!

Nothing more was said until they'd reached her flat. Jake got out of the car, slamming the door behind him and locking it. "Come on," he said grimly, taking her arm and going to the apartment block.

At her front door Debbie said, "Well, I'll say goodnight to you, Blair—"

"Oh, no, you won't," Jake said, shaking his head. "And don't call me Blair. This isn't Blair, whom you can use as a doormat because he's Lucky Driver's paid gofer.

This is Jake, who's nobody's doormat. I'm spelling it out because I want to get the ground rules clear before the fight starts.''

"Fight? What fight?"

"You know perfectly well what fight. The one we've been spoiling for from the first moment."

Debbie's eyes gleamed. "Right. You're on."

As soon as the apartment door was closed behind them they stripped off their outdoor clothing, tossing it aside to stand facing each other like two boxers after "Seconds out!"

"Any more ground rules?" Debbie demanded.

"Just one. We start out by getting it clear what we're fighting about."

Debbie's eyes flashed with eager anticipation. "Who cares, as long as it's a good fight?"

At these words a curious sensation came over Jake. How often, and in how many varied situations, had he thought precisely the same, but suppressed it in the interests of propriety? How many women in the world understood the thrill of a really satisfying bust-up? And what kindly fate had sent this one his way?

"Well, we have all the excuse we need," he said. "I have had you up to here, Miss Harker. I've had it with you ordering me around, your snide remarks and your assumption that you can walk over me anytime you choose."

"But I *can* walk over you, Jake," she assured him. "As long as I have Lucky behind me, that's just what I can do."

"Don't get drunk with power," he warned her. "Lucky won't always be behind you, and when this is over—"

"When this is over the situation between us will have changed out of all recognition," Debbie said.

His eyes narrowed. "And just what do you mean by that?"

"I mean exactly the same as you do, when you say it to yourself."

She understood too much, he thought angrily. It was unnerving that she actually knew the things he said to himself. "Let's stick to now," he growled. "Just because some second-rate gangster thinks you're the bee's knees—"

"Which is what you always wanted him to think, thus proving that I'm doing my job properly—"

"Job?" he echoed bitterly. "You're not doing a job. You're enjoying yourself."

"Of course I am. I believe in combining business with pleasure. I'm having a whale of a time." She regarded him innocently. "Aren't you?"

"No. But then, I'm not as two-faced as you are."

That got her good'n mad, he was delighted to note. She glared at him, eyes sparkling with annoyance. "Two-faced? How dare you insult me!"

"Now, look—"

"Only *two* faces? I have a dozen," she told him indignantly. "In this job I wouldn't last five minutes with a mere two."

"Oh, really! Tell me about these faces."

"Do I need to? You've already seen some of them for yourself. I can be whatever's needed, a stripper for Elroy Speke, a brainless bimbo for the customers, a classy dame for Lucky. I can be an efficient secretary, a sporty lady with a passion for tennis. I've got a sharp tongue or a sweet one, depending on the requirements. I've got a face for every part. All I need is the directions."

Jake glowered like a man at the end of his tether, and suddenly Debbie's teasing smile died, because she'd seen something in his look that made her heart beat. The next moment he reached out, pulling her into his arms. "And which face are you wearing now?" he asked, lowering his head as he spoke.

Although she was expecting it, the touch of his mouth came as a shock. His kiss had lived on her lips since the day they'd met, tormenting her dreams and her waking thoughts, and making every meeting an endurance test of frustration. She'd thought she remembered how he felt under her hands, but now she realized how wrong she'd been. This was no memory but a real man, warm and living, kissing her with a fierce desperation that told her he, too, had been suffering. His lips were hard on hers, moving with a driving purposefulness that was exactly how she'd imagined it, how she'd wanted it. She let her body relax, yielding herself up blissfully to the sweet, hot excitement that streamed through her. She'd yearned for this, and now she was going to enjoy it to the full.

Neither his best friends nor his worst enemies would have called Jake a "new man." In his mind this was no meeting of equals but an explosion of wrath. He was going to teach her a lesson, show her how mistaken she was to think she could taunt him with impunity.

But something was wrong. He knew that as soon as he felt the laughter shaking her body. "What's so damned funny?" he demanded against her mouth.

"You are," she murmured.

"You think this is funny? Lady, you've seen nothing yet." The last word was muffled as the tip of her tongue flickered against his lips, making it impossible for him to do anything but smother her mouth again, growling with anger and something else that he couldn't define, but which scared him because he wasn't used to it.

"You want me, Jake," she whispered. "You've always wanted me."

"Quiet!"

"But it's true, isn't it? It's always been there—for both of us—from the first moment."

"You flatter yourself."

"You're a coward, Jake," she murmured against his mouth. "You can't face the truth."

Hell might freeze over but no one could call Jake Garfield a coward. With one swift movement he lifted her in his arms and held her tight, her face close to his. "Take that back," he commanded.

She regarded him with impish defiance. "Make me."

"Right." He kicked open the bedroom door. "Put the light on."

"No, it's nicer this way."

"Put the light on," he said desperately. "I can't find the damned bed in the dark."

She switched on a small bedside lamp. The next moment her arms were about his neck and her lips on his. The sweetness of the sensation went through him so powerfully that he lost his footing and deposited them both on the bed. They landed, clutching each other somehow, anyhow, but still managing to keep their lips in contact. Debbie tightened her arms about Jake and he drew her close, taking control of the kiss. She relaxed, knowing instinctively that she was in the hands of a master. This was a man with a sense of purpose in everything he did and the knowledge made her feel good. Her excitement was rising fast and when he slid his tongue between her lips she opened for him at once, eager for the thrusting, urgent movements against the inside of her mouth.

He'd kissed her at their first meeting, but this kiss was different. On that day he'd been cynically taking what was offered, scornful of the woman who offered it. But now he was relating to *her,* Debbie Harker, a woman who drove him mad but whom he couldn't get out from under his skin. He wanted to seduce her and be seduced by her, because nobody else would do. All this was there in the slow, determined caresses of his mouth and the way he explored her deeply and satisfyingly.

His fingers moved swiftly, opening her buttons to reveal the naked breasts beneath. They were rich and ripe, and already the nipples peaked proudly at the approach of the triumph for which she'd schemed for weeks. They would tell him all he wanted to know, except that he knew it already. It was understood between them that they'd been on fire for each other from the first moment. No words were needed. No denials, no conditions, no admissions, just *yes*.

He didn't tell her she was beautiful, but then, why should he? The shortness of his temper had been telling her that from the beginning. But his eyes told her things his lips could never have found the words for. And his tongue told her again when it traced a pattern over one white breast to curl lovingly around the nipple. A long, luxurious sigh escaped her. It was so good, and it promised her so much. She could hardly wait for the rest, but she controlled her impatience, too proud to let him know that her craving was as great as his own.

He had a wicked mouth, full of subtle skill to torment and delight her, and he used it with slow deliberation. Fire went through her whenever he touched her nipple with the tip of his tongue. The whole world seemed to be ablaze, with herself as the heart of the fire, content to burn up into oblivion and be reborn. Yet when he drew back and looked down on the picture she presented she managed to be sufficiently mistress of herself to ask, "Am I what you wanted?"

"You know damned well that you are," he growled. "You've been planning this, haven't you?"

"No more than you."

"And I walked right into it, didn't I?"

She answered him, not in words but in a deep-throated chuckle that was his undoing. He began to tear off his clothes and found, when he'd finished, that her clothes, too, lay somewhere on the floor. Her body glowed with warmth and silky beauty, sliding easily into his arms and pressing urgently against his own.

Now the time for words was past. Debbie's breath came fast as he caressed her urgently, igniting flames of excitement that roared along her nerves. She was melting in the fierceness of her own passion as it blended with his, becoming a new element that was beyond both of them. This was more than passion. It was a recognition of something that had been inevitable since time began, and which was drawing them into an unimaginable closeness.

She wanted that closeness with all her heart, yet now that it was here she knew a moment of apprehension. Despite appearances she lived an austere life in the privacy of her own home. In the two years since she'd moved into this apartment, Jake was the first man to get as far as her bed. She had taken a gamble, and was about to discover whether it would pay off.

His movements changed. He was asking her silently if she was ready for him, and she responded by parting her legs in welcome. She gave a small gasp at the unfamiliar sensation as he slid into her slowly, with restrained power. He was trembling with urgency, but he claimed her as if he had all the time in the world, giving her time to respond. Jake might be rough and tough on the surface, but he knew things about a woman's body, and how to treat it, that only a man of sensitivity and style could have known. He retreated slightly, then drove back into her, still slowly, watching her face for any sign that all wasn't well. But there was no such sign. All was well. It would always be well while she could blend her body with this man's, relaxing in the utter certainty of his skill.

Her mantle of confidence was cast away from her now. The feeling of being one with him was changing her from the inside, showing her the world in new colors. They were beautiful, dark and stormy, searing red, orange, yellow; the colors of fire, shot through with glittering white and yellow, like the explosions of rockets. They seemed to zoom up into the firmament, dazzling her with wonder.

She felt consumed by pleasure, engulfed, buffeted and filled by it. He was moving vigorously, driving her to the moment of release at heady speed. What little control she had left slipped away. She clung to him as the rockets exploded, spinning them both upward too fast to breathe, then tossing them around in a whirlwind. A long cry broke from her. It was part ecstatic pleasure, but also part frustration that what had been so fulfilling and satisfying was so soon over. The colors changed from red to violet, to blue, and finally to the soft greens of repose.

Gasping slightly, they lay side by side, heads turned to regard each other. "So that's that?" Debbie ventured.

"Uh-huh." His reply was noncommittal, his eyes wary.

"I mean, we always knew that we had to get it out of the way."

"That's right."

"And we did."

"And we did."

"Like two sensible adults."

"Indubitably!"

"So now we've removed the obstacle and it won't bother us anymore."

At last he exploded. *"Quit yakking woman, and come back here this instant."*

Gleefully she threw herself into his open arms, and it was there again, as sweet and urgent as the first time, but with the new edge of experience to guide them to greater heights.

Now she knew the power of his hard, lean body, honed and made ready for action by the tough life he led. There was a scar on one shoulder where a bullet had caught him and a place on his chest where the hair no longer grew properly, the relic of a knife wound. To Debbie these were not blemishes but symbols of the active life that was essential to her, both for herself and a man she might love. They marked him out as her man, a man with a primitive streak, that many women would have shunned, but that was meat and drink to her.

This time she was ready for him early, almost pulling him inside her in her eagerness to have what only he could give. She thrust up to meet him in a fierce movement that she could tell surprised him. Delighted, she did it again and was thrilled by his gasp of pleasure. After that there was nothing to choose between them as they drove each other onward to the finishing line, crossing it triumphantly together.

After passion came sleep; stunned, satiated, luxurious sleep, with the two of them lying motionless in each other's arms like children. Debbie awoke to find herself lying in exactly the same position as when she'd dropped off. She thought back to the restless nights when she'd tossed and turned, tormented by the unattainable memory of Jake's body. Now, for the first time in weeks, she felt utterly relaxed and contented. Jake, too, looked as if he'd slept without moving, his arms twined around her, his face at peace. She drew her fingers along his arm and he awoke.

As soon as he saw her he was smiling, not cynically as she'd seen so often before, but as if he really meant it. "Which face are you wearing now?" he asked softly.

"This is the cat that swallowed the cream," she purred.

"I guess we both found something out."

She yawned and stretched in delicious satisfaction. "Not a bit," she said. "*You* found something out. *I* knew it all the time."

He grinned. "Well, do you think I didn't?"

"You'd have died before admitting it."

"There are some things that a man's better off not admitting if he values his safety. You came labeled Danger in big lettering—"

"You *are* a coward," she said triumphantly. "I knew it."

"I'm not a coward," he said firmly. "But a wise man reconnoiters the terrain before moving in to take over."

"Oh, you think you're going to take over?"

"That's how I like it."

"Well, you're welcome to try," she murmured.

Her smile challenged him, and his heart somersaulted at the thought of the coming tussle. To calm himself down he concentrated on something prosaic. "I ought to get up and get to work."

"Work? Good heavens, it's morning." For the first time Debbie realized how light the room was.

"That's right. We slept a long time."

"I guess that's no surprise," she teased. She kissed him, then threw herself back luxuriously. "To hell with work. Lucky's away, remember."

"It's better if he doesn't call in and find me missing."

She kept a firm hold on him, reluctant to let this new delight slip away so soon. "If Lucky calls you could tell him you were keeping an eye on me, protecting me from the attentions of other men," she said mischievously.

He grinned but then became serious again and said, "I wish I could have gone with him. Just think what I might be learning."

"It doesn't matter. I've got a plan for finding out plenty."

"What?" he asked with sudden misgiving.

"I'm going to make Lucky tell me everything."

He grimaced. "For a moment I thought you were serious."

"I *am* serious," she said indignantly. "Don't you remember how Lucky opened up when he got upset? He's an emotional man and when he gets het up he becomes indiscreet. So I've got to make him indiscreet again."

"And how are you going to do that?"

"Pick a quarrel with him, get him angry. It's actually very simple."

Jake groaned. "I've heard Manners complaining about the things that look simple to you. According to him they shortened his life by about ten years."

"Manners had no imagination."

"I envy him. Unfortunately I do have imagination, enough to go white-haired at the thought of you deliberately provoking such a dangerous man into a quarrel."

"He's not dangerous with me," Debbie said lightly.

"For God's sake, stop saying things like that!" Jake pleaded. "You don't know what you're talking about."

"I know that when Lucky's good'n mad he talks."

"So you're going to make him mad at you? Do you know what happens to people Lucky gets mad with? They get hurt—or dead."

"Well, what does that matter as long as I find something out?" Debbie asked practically.

Jake tore his hair, biting back all the things he wanted to say. He was horribly aware of being divided in two. The policeman part of him applauded her ingenuity and her courage. The lover wanted to beg her to take no chances. But she had opportunities he lacked. That was the brutal truth of it.

"Perhaps if we plan it carefully..." he began.

"Oh, that's all taken care of," she said in an airy manner that filled him with foreboding. "Do you remember that song Harry wrote me?"

"'My Kind Of Man'?" Jake remembered. "I've seen you rehearsing it, haven't I?"

"Not the way I'm going to perform it when Lucky gets back," Debbie said with a chuckle. "I got bored one day when there was a holdup in the rehearsal, and to pass the time I wrote some new words."

"What kind of words?" he asked uneasily.

"Well—a bit naughty. I'm going to substitute my words for Harry's, with appropriate actions. I'll show you."

She leapt to her feet and ran into the bathroom. She never did anything slowly, Jake realized, unless it was part of the role she was playing. As Silver she could saunter seductively, showing off her beauty, but when she was being herself everything was done in a rush of explosive energy. After a moment she reappeared with a towel draped around her.

"This is me, making my entrance through the curtains," she said. "And I stand a moment, gazing out at the audience while the music plays. Then I come down to the microphone...." She moved languidly forward, keeping her eyes on Jake beneath heavy lashes. "And I start to sing...."

She assumed a husky growl. "I'm looking for...my kind of man.... He must be—" she smiled at Jake "—*all* man."

Despite his worries, Jake grinned. She was brilliant. He had to give her that.

Debbie allowed the towel to slip a little, still keeping Jake caught in her dazzling headlights. "We'll do everything together," she intoned throatily. "He can touch me on my hair—and there—and any other where..."

Jake's forehead was damp. The words were only mildly suggestive, but she infused them with an erotic tension from deep within herself that made him feel as if he was on fire.

She came closer, lifting one long leg, placing the pointed foot daintily on the bed beside him and rocking back and forth. The towel was clinging on by faith and prayer—where it *was* clinging. "I like a man of many parts," she crooned, tracing a finger down his cheek, "but not too much heart...." Her fingertips were skittering over his chest. "It gets in the way—of business."

"You're going to do this to Lucky in the middle of a performance?" Jake said raggedly.

"Oh, no, not Lucky. I'll pick a likely looking man from one of the front tables. Lucky won't be able to do a thing about it. Do you think it will be effective?"

Jake was beyond speech. With one movement he yanked the towel from her and threw it into a corner. Then he tossed her onto her back and seized her wrists. "You're mad," he managed to say. "Stark, staring, raving mad."

She lay there, laughing up at him. "Tell me about it, Jake."

He looked down into her teasing face and something happened to him that had nothing to do with the thunder in his blood or the turmoil in his loins. She was ready to walk so merrily into deadly danger and his heart responded with an aching delight. What a comrade to have beside him on a fearsome road! What a joy! What a beauty! What a woman!

"Why should I become the millionth person to tell you how crazy you are?" he growled. "What notice do you ever take? You're not going to do this. Never. Not in a million years. It looks like a wonderful plan, but it's full of holes."

"Name one."

"You don't know what Lucky will do when he gets really mad. He might kill you. It's no good him spilling the beans if you're too dead to tell me about them."

She appeared much struck by this. "That's true, Jake, and there's only one thing for us to do."

"Right. We abandon the whole scheme."

"You'll have to be listening outside the door so that you can take notes of anything he says. Then it won't matter if he kills me," she finished triumphantly.

He tore his hair. "Debbie, I forbid this."

"Get lost."

"Debbie—"

"Listen, Detective Inspector, are you seriously going to order me off our best chance of a breakthrough? What are you, a professional policeman or an amateur who quits when it gets tough?"

"I do not quit when it gets tough," he said through gritted teeth.

"Then don't insult me by expecting me to do any different. Now, it's time you got dressed and went to work."

Six

———

They were still arguing next day, when Jake drove her to the club in the early evening. "I think it's about time you dropped the subject," Debbie muttered as they walked down the corridor to her dressing room. "I've made up my mind."

"Then you'd better change it before Lucky comes back tomorrow," he muttered back.

But a shock was waiting for them both. Debbie got the first warning as she opened her door and saw the dressing room massed with white roses. *"Surprise,"* Lucky sang out, appearing from behind the door. "Didn't expect me for another day, huh? But I just couldn't keep away from you."

"Darling!" Debbie threw her arms around him. "How lovely to see you."

"Wait till you see what I brought you!" With a flourish he produced a jewelry box. Jake made himself scarce without waiting to see what it contained. As he strode down the corridor he tried not to think of what was going on behind that door. Lucky's ardor had brought him speeding back, bearing gifts. What would he demand as a welcome? Sweat stood out on Jake's brow. It had been bad enough when he'd been able to view the problem academically— *almost* academically. But that was way back, at least two days ago. She was his now.

It seemed an endless time until Lucky appeared in the club, self-consciously wiping lipstick from his mouth. "Evening, Jake," he sang out cheerfully.

Jake kept his face and voice expressionless. "Good evening, Mr. Driver. I hope you had a successful visit."

"Fine, thank you. Now I can't wait to see my lady perform. She says she's got a very special surprise for me tonight."

Cold shivers ran down Jake's spine. She was going to do it. The crazy female had picked tonight of all nights to drive this killer up the wall. He muttered an excuse and hurried away, trying not to run.

She was just putting the finishing touches to her makeup and surveying Lucky's gift, which glittered on her wrist. "Isn't it pretty?" she said.

"It's probably hot," Jake snapped. "You'll have to give it back. In fact, after tonight he'll probably snatch it back, if you're going to do what I think you are."

"Oh, I'm going to do it, all right. There'll never be a better night than tonight."

"Why?"

"Because he's eager and ardent, certain that I love him."

"So?"

"Well, can you think of a better time to kick him in the teeth?" she asked innocently.

Rationally, he couldn't. The policeman in him applauded her courage. The man knew a moment's pity for Lucky, a pawn at the mercy of this scheming siren. And the lover wondered what the hell he'd got himself into here. "You are doing this against my advice," he growled.

"As long as I'm doing it, that's all that matters. Close the door behind you, *Blair.*"

Jake was on hot coals throughout the floor show, hoping, without much confidence, that Debbie wouldn't go over the top. Lucky appeared just before her entrance, and positioned himself, leaning against a wall, where he could get a good view of her.

At last the lights dimmed. There was a roll of drums, a brilliant spotlight shone onto a curtain of pure glitter and the next moment Debbie was standing there. She was magnificent in her shimmering silver dress with its plunging neck and high-slit thigh. She waited a moment, arms uplifted to acknowledge the applause. At last she began to descend the stairs until she reached the front of the stage. The smile she gave the audience produced roars of delight. It was slow, luxurious and full of promise. Lucky was grinning with approval.

But his grin faded as Debbie began to croon, "I'm looking for...my kind of man." She stepped off the stage and shimmered closer to the front row of tables. Behind the smoochy manner her eyes were alert as they scanned the men and finally came to rest on one in particular. He was in his forties, handsome in a vulgar, obvious way, and his lips were wet because he continually licked them. "He must be—*all* man," she sang huskily, leaning toward him and tickling his face. He grinned his delight, while two other men at the same table roared their approval. As he made a grab for her she glided away to one of the others.

"We'll do *everything* together." When the second man reached for her, she sat in his lap. "He can touch me on my hair—and there—and *any other* where..." she crooned, suppressing her disgust at the smell of booze and sweat that came from him. The audience was in uproar, laughing and cheering. Lucky's lips were still stretched in the shape of a smile, but the life had drained out from behind it and his eyes were like stones.

The third man at the table grabbed Debbie's hand and she switched her attention to this new prey. "I like a man of many parts, but not too much heart... it gets in the way—of business."

Watching Lucky's dead, cruel face, Jake knew that his reluctance to work with a woman had been right. In the end it always came to this. If you had a shred of liking, respect or affection for the woman, you ended up terrified for her. When he thought of some of the uglier stories he'd heard about Lucky and saw the way he was looking at Debbie, Jake's blood froze.

The third man had seized Debbie's hand and was kissing it as if he would devour it. Brian, who was standing next to Lucky, made a movement as if to spring forward, but Lucky held up a restraining hand, as if saying that he would deal with this himself. But he stayed where he was. Only his eyes moved, following Debbie as she freed herself and returned to the stage, laughing and acknowledging the audience's applause.

When the show was over she went quickly to her dressing room. She didn't want to fight with Lucky wearing the impractical stage costume, and she'd managed to discard it and put on slacks and a sweater by the time he came to her. She was sitting at the dressing table removing her makeup with an air of unconcern when he burst in.

She knew immediately that she'd been successful. Lucky's face was pale and sweating, and it twitched slightly. "That was a nice little performance you put on tonight, sweetie," he said, but there was no affection in his tone.

"It was quite something, wasn't it?" she agreed with a little giggle. "I worked really hard on getting it right."

His cheek twitched. "Oh, you worked hard, did you? You really thought about making a fool of me?"

"Making a fool of you? I don't know what you mean, Lucky." She was excited to notice that he was fast losing control.

"Like hell you don't!"

Debbie turned wide, innocent eyes on him, rightly calculating that the sense of failing to get through to her would inflame him further. "But I thought you'd be pleased," she pouted.

"Oh, sure I was pleased!" Lucky said savagely. "I was real *pleased* to see you draping yourself over other men, letting them paw you about."

"But you like other men to want me, you said so."

"Want you, yes, but at a distance. They can want as much as they like but *you belong to me.* You knew that." He turned away from her, running a hand through his hair. "You knew. How could you be so stupid? Oh, the hell!"

He gave a long sigh. With dismay Debbie realized that he was actually calming down. Evidently her power over him was stronger than she'd thought. In another moment he'd be forgiving her, and that would never do. "Don't ever say I belong you to, Lucky," she said sharply. "Because it's not true. Maybe it's a good thing for you to be reminded of that."

FREE BOOKS!

FREE GIFTS!

Play the "Lucky 7" Slot Machine Game!

NO COST! NO OBLIGATION TO BUY! NO PURCHASE NECESSARY!

PLAY "LUCKY 7"
AND GET AS MANY AS SIX FREE GIFTS...

HOW TO PLAY:

1 With a coin, carefully scratch away the silver panel opposite. Then check the claim chart to see what we have for you - FREE BOOKS and gifts - ALL YOURS! ALL FREE!

2 When you return this card we'll send you specially selected Silhouette Desires and the gifts you qualify for, absolutely FREE. There's no catch. You're under no obligation to buy anything. We charge nothing for your first shipment. And you don't have to make any minimum number of purchases.

3 After you've received your FREE books, if we don't hear from you, we will send you six brand new Silhouette Desires to read and enjoy every month for just £2.20* each - the same price as the books in the shops. There is no extra charge for postage and packing and no hidden extras.

4 The fact is thousands of readers enjoy receiving books through the post from the Reader Service. They like the convenience of home delivery... they like getting the best new novels at least a month before they're available in the shops... and they love their subscriber Newsletter, featuring author news, horoscopes, penfriends, competitions and much more.

5 We hope that after receiving your free books you'll want to remain a subscriber. But the choice is yours - to continue or cancel, anytime at all! So why not take up our invitation - you'll be glad you did!

*Prices subject to change without notice.

You'll look like a million dollars when you wear this lovely necklace! Its cobra-link chain is a generous 18" long, and the multi-faceted Austrian crystal sparkles like a diamond!

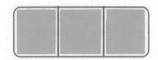

Play "Lucky 7"

2S6SD

Just scratch away the silver panel with a coin.
Then check below to see how many FREE GIFTS will be yours.

YES! I have scratched away the silver panel. Please send me all the gifts for which I qualify. I understand that I am under no obligation to purchase any books, as explained on the opposite page. I am over 18 years of age.

BLOCK CAPITALS PLEASE

MS/MRS/MISS/MR _____

ADDRESS _____

_____

POSTCODE _____

 WORTH FOUR FREE BOOKS
PLUS A NECKLACE AND MYSTERY GIFT

 WORTH FOUR FREE BOOKS
PLUS A MYSTERY GIFT

 WORTH FOUR FREE BOOKS

 WORTH TWO FREE BOOKS

READER SERVICE 'NO RISK' GUARANTEE

SILHOUETTE READER SERVICE
FREEPOST
Croydon
Surrey
CR9 3WZ

NO
STAMP
NEEDED

That got him, she was relieved to see. His face became an ugly mottled purple. "Why you—get this into your head. You belong to me because I've bought and paid for you."

"I told you—"

"No, *I'm* telling *you.* I've spent a fortune on you. I've put up with your moods and the way you give me the cold shoulder, because I admired you." Rage was overtaking him fast. "I skipped a meeting with Rox Leverham to get back here. His stuff's the best in the business, and I made him wait, for *you.* I've offended people by telling them to stay away because they were too coarse for you. Dan Sedgewick didn't like that one bit and that's a man who can do me a lot of harm, but I did it for you." His voice rose to a shriek. *"Only you've got to be exclusively mine, do you understand?"*

Jake, hovering in the corridor just outside, was making frantic notes of these indiscretions with one half of his brain. The other half was dizzy with admiration for a colleague who'd brought off the difficult trick, while at the same time sending up frantic prayers for her safety.

Suddenly there was a loud crash, followed by a woman's scream. It took every ounce of discipline Jake possessed not to rush in there and defend her. Fear and anger curdled in his stomach and he coped in the only way that he could—by projecting it all onto her.

Stupid woman! he raged inwardly. *She's gone too far. She'll blow it by driving him over the top. Trust her to make a mess of it.*

The dressing room door opened suddenly and Debbie came flying out. Tears were pouring down her face but to Jake's relief she appeared unhurt. "I hate you, Lucky," she sobbed. "How could you turn on me when I was just trying to do my best for you?"

Through the open door Jake could see the mirror, smashed to pieces as if something had been thrown violently against it. Lucky appeared in the doorway. His shirt had been torn open, revealing a glistening, heaving chest, his hair was disheveled and there was a manic light in his eyes.

"Get out of here, you lousy tart!" he screamed. "Get out and don't come back. If I see you in this place again—" His voice rose to a demented scream. *"I'll kill you."*

Debbie fled down the corridor. Lucky stayed where he was, his whole body quivering with hate and fury. *"I'll kill you—I'll kill you."*

Jake backed into the shadows, fighting down his instinct to go after Debbie, because that would be unprofessional. And also because she would never forgive him. Even when Lucky strode after her down the corridor, still shouting, Jake restrained himself with a huge effort.

By slipping out of one side entrance and in through another he managed to return to the main area of the club without being seen. The guests had gone and the waiters were starting to clear up. Jake mingled with them and began collecting glasses from tables and returning them to the bar. In the corner he could see Lucky having a furious conversation with Brian. Lucky looked up and saw him. "Jake. Where the hell have you been? Why aren't you there when I want you?"

"Sorry, Mr. Driver. Just doing a little clearing up."

"Get the car out." He turned on his heel.

Brian met Jake's eye. There was a look of sneering pleasure on his face. "I guess that stupid bitch has blown it this time," he said.

He got no further. Lucky, returning unexpectedly, had overheard Brian's words and felled him to the ground with one blow. "Don't you ever talk like that about her," he screamed. "D'you hear?"

Blood was pouring from Brian's nose and he was actually shaking with fear. "Yes, Mr. D-driver..." he stammered.

Lucky was growing demented. "You're a cheap nothing," he shouted. "You're not fit to lick her boots." He turned his fire on Jake. "I told you to get the car."

Jake brought the Rolls to the entrance. Lucky got into the back seat, slammed the door and said, "Anywhere!"

For the first ten minutes he sat in the back, a grim, brooding presence, muttering, "The bitch! The cheap, lousy bitch!" in a voice that was half a spit. Suddenly he snapped, "Step on it. D'you call this driving?"

"I'm over the speed limit already, Mr. Driver."

"Stop the car."

Jake pulled over and Lucky got into the driver's seat. For the next fifteen minutes Lucky took out his rage on the steering wheel, while Jake watched the speedometer with mounting fascination. At last Lucky swung back and did the return journey in a more controlled manner. Jake realized with misgiving that they were heading for Debbie's apartment.

Debbie went home by taxi. For the first part of the journey she was madly scribbling notes of everything Lucky had spilled in his fury. When she'd finished she looked out the rear window, but there was no sign of pursuit. Inwardly she was singing with triumph. It had worked.

Once in her apartment she plunged into the shower, luxuriating in the feeling of the clean water laving her as she washed off the heat and smoke of the nightclub, the tension, the pressure of hate and anger and male hands grabbing. They'd sickened her but she'd gone through with it to the end. Each nerve had been alert during that outrageous song and she'd had the impression of seeing everything at once: the lustful faces of the men she was inciting, Lucky's look of suppressed rage.

But there'd been something else, more than all these, that had burned into her consciousness. Jake's expression had been that of a man in agony; not merely disgust at seeing her play the coquette, but horror and fear for the consequences, fear for *her*.

She remembered how he'd been in her bed, fierce and powerful yet sometimes unexpectedly tender. He was a man to whom tenderness didn't come easily, but it was there, waiting for the right woman to bring it out. Their second lovemaking had been sweeter than the first. They knew each other by then, with the deep, wordless understanding of the flesh, knew that they could risk discarding their wariness and trusting each other.

Thinking of him was making her dizzy. Every pore of her was alive with memory. If only he would come to her now. Their lovemaking had slaked her passion only briefly. Before that she'd wanted him, but in ignorance. Now there was a new deprivation, deeper than ever because it grew out of knowledge. He'd made her body complete, and now incompleteness was unbearable.

The soap slipped through her fingers. She made a grab, missed it and shrugged. Suds poured down her in streams as the water rinsed her and she gave a sigh of pure physical delight. At last she was finished. She turned off the water and reached out for the shower door. At that moment her foot found the missing soap. She slithered, clutching frantically, still half-blinded by water, unable to save herself. The collision with the tiled wall was like a fist punching her head.

* * *

Jake put his finger on Debbie's bell and kept it there for several seconds. When he'd finished he could hear her on the other side. "Who is it?" she called cautiously.

"It's only me. I'm alone."

She let him in and he closed the door behind him. He had a thousand things to say but every single one went out of his head when he saw her. "Dear God!" he exploded. "He hit you! The bastard hit you!"

"No—Jake—"

"I was outside listening. I didn't see . . . when you left the dressing room the corridor was too dark for. . . I never saw . . ."

The ugly bruise on the side of her face was already an interesting color. Jake touched it with light fingers, swearing under his breath all the time.

"Jake it's all right, really, I—"

"Shut up," he said, not rudely but like a man who was maintaining his concentration. "I'll kill the bastard for this."

Debbie stared at him, her attention caught by something in his face that she'd never seen before. He was shaking and there was a tremor in his voice. Nor had she ever known anything like the gentleness with which he touched her face. Slowly he drew her closer to him and laid his lips against the bruise so softly that she felt no pain, only the sweetness of his mouth's pressure. "I shouldn't have let you do it," he murmured. "I knew it was madness. It was too great a risk. He might have killed you. . . .dear God!"

She was melting inside and her heart ached, wanting the lovely moment to go on and on. But her innate honesty got in the way of even a temporary deception. "Jake," she said unsteadily, "it's all right."

"It's not all right," he said at once. "It's not all right for anyone to hurt you."

"But he didn't—"

"Darling, you're sweet and brave but that's a nasty bruise. What did he hit you with? His fist? I'm going to see him put away for the rest of his life—"

She tried to speak but he silenced her with his lips on hers. Calling up all her resolution, she forced herself to push him away. It was the hardest thing she'd ever done. "Lucky never touched me," she said.

"Why do you defend him? I can *see* that he hit you—"

"He didn't," she said desperately. "I fell."

"You mean, he pushed you. That's just as bad—"

"I mean, Lucky had nothing to do with it. I slipped on the soap in the shower since I got home. I fell and hit my head on the wall."

He didn't move. It was as though a stream of ice was going through his body, freezing every part. At last he said, "Is that for real? You're not kidding me?"

"No kidding. I just fell in the shower."

He stood back. "Well," he said in a forced voice, "I had visions of Lucky punching you. That's a relief—at least—it's not a relief that you're hurt, but I'm glad that—"

"It's all right, Jake," she said brightly. "I know what you mean."

It was a disaster, she realized. She'd tried to tell him the truth but she hadn't been fast enough. Now he felt foolish, and he would keep his distance. But she'd seen something in his eyes she wanted to go on seeing, and his embarrassment hurt her.

Jake went into the kitchen and started making coffee. He didn't want coffee but it was something to do with his hands, so that he didn't have to look at her and see his own idiocy reflected in her eyes. He thought of the things he'd said. "It's not all right for anyone to hurt you... Darling, you're sweet and brave...." He'd called her *darling*. He'd actually said the word, with all its implications. Thank heaven, he hadn't made an even bigger fool of himself.

He cast a discreet glance at her, sitting by the window, seemingly unaware of him. She looked up at him and smiled. It was a tentative smile, as if she was wondering if he were offended. He realized that it was the first touch of uncertainty he'd ever seen in her, and it caused something strange to happen to his heart. His embarrassment of a moment ago was forgotten. What did it matter beside the fact that she was injured?

"You should be in bed," he said, going to sit beside her. He touched the bruise gently. "It's a nasty one. You've got a headache."

"I didn't say so."

"I can see it."

"I don't want to go to bed," she said rebelliously. She let the edges of her bathrobe fall apart, revealing a sight that strained his self-discipline to the utmost. "At least, I do—but not to sleep," she added enticingly.

"Well, you'll just have to control yourself," he told her, trying to speak severely and not quite managing it. His blood was rioting in his veins. "Come along. Bed and sleep. You're not well."

"That's true, I'm not," she said with a sigh. "In fact, I feel suddenly weak. Why don't you carry me to bed?"

He knew her game. She thought once he had her in his arms there'd be no stopping him. But she'd misjudged her man. It was torture but he picked her up, took her into the bedroom and laid her on the bed as platonically as a

brother. The slight twitch of her lips told him she understood everything that was happening inside him, and although her eyes were dark with pain they still contained
mockery.

"What happened after I'd gone?" she asked as he
tucked her up.

"Lucky told me to get the car out and drive. I didn't go
fast enough for him so he took the wheel himself and I've
never had such a hair-raising time. Then he headed back
here. I was afraid he was coming to see you but instead he
dropped me outside your apartment and drove off. I've
been set to spy on you. I'm to watch night and day. If you
go out I'm to follow you and if anyone visits you here I'm
to let him know at once."

As if in confirmation Jake's mobile phone rang. He laid
a finger over his lips and answered it. Debbie could just
make out Lucky's voice, tinny and disembodied. "I've
just got back. Have you seen any sign of her?"

"Not yet, boss," Jake replied.

"You mean, she's not there at all?"

"Oh, yes, she's there," Jake said quickly. "I saw lights
on in her apartment, then they all went out, so I guess
she's asleep."

"Do you need some help on this assignment? Shall I
send Brian?"

"No need. I'm fine," Jake said quickly.

"Remember, I want to know everything that bitch
does."

"Everything," Jake promised. He shut the phone off
and breathed out hard. "This isn't going to be easy," he
said.

When Debbie didn't answer he looked down and saw
that she'd fallen asleep. She looked pale and weary. An

inner compulsion made him lean down and kiss her forehead. "You crazy woman," he murmured.

So who isn't crazy? asked the voice in his head. *You?*

Moving very gently, he put his arm on the headboard and leaned over her in an attitude of watchfulness and protection.

And he smiled to himself as he realized how cross that would make her.

Seven

Debbie awoke to find herself wrapped in Jake's arms. He was lying on the outside of the bedclothes, but somehow he'd contrived to get one arm beneath her and one over her. The bed wasn't quite big enough for a double, and they were pressed close together, except for the bedclothes in between.

She wriggled over onto her back, moving slowly, so as not to awaken him. His face was very close to hers, and she studied it sleeping as she had done once before. But now everything was different. Now she knew him intimately. It wasn't just that she was familiar with his body: that was the easy part. But last night she'd had a glimpse into his heart. It had been a fluke, an accident, and he'd let her in reluctantly. But what she'd discovered had made her own heart glow.

She knew now that the gentler face he showed in sleep was a real part of him, and not merely an accidental relaxation of muscles. Behind the abruptness of his manner and the harshness of his life there was a man with the power to touch her innermost feelings. Since the first meeting she'd wanted him physically, but that was as nothing compared to the way she wanted him now.

She found it oddly touching that he was lying outside the bedclothes, fully dressed. After the raging of their passion he might have come under the covers with her and held her naked body against his own. That was what many men would have done. But this man evidently had a streak of delicacy that forbade him to take anything for granted while she was asleep and injured. It was the last thing she would have expected of him. She began to think it might take all her life to know him well, but it would be worth it. On the thought she fell asleep again.

When she awoke he was gone but she could hear movement in the kitchen. He appeared a moment later with a tray bearing coffee and rolls, which he set on the bed beside her. "Eat it all up," he said. "You've got to get your strength back."

"Mmm, lovely," she said, pulling herself up in bed. "It's so long since I was spoiled by breakfast in bed."

He regarded her tenderly as she spread honey on the rolls and devoured them as eagerly as a schoolgirl. With her hair in disarray and her glorious face scrubbed clean of makeup, she looked younger than he'd ever seen her. When she'd finished he removed the tray and asked, "How's your head this morning?"

"I'm as fit as a fiddle. I could get up and do anything."

"That's the point. You can't do anything, not without me following to report back to Lucky. Why not have a day in bed?"

"Yum, yum!" she said at once, regarding him with an eagerness that made him laugh.

"I meant, recovering your strength," he said.

"I'm perfectly strong. Let me show you." Without warning, she pounced, tickling him unmercifully.

"Hey, get off!" he yelled, but her fingers were everywhere, and he didn't really want to push her away. So he defeated her by another means, getting both his arms about her and trapping her against his chest, yet holding her gently all the while.

"I don't want you to take any risks with your head," he said.

She lay in his arms in a state of utter contentment. "Do you mean to tell me that you're going to hold me like this and not make love to me?" she demanded with impish humor.

"Yes," he said firmly.

"Are you sure you can manage it?"

"Yes, damn it."

"Liar," she teased.

"What about all that self-control we promised ourselves?" he demanded.

"It's a myth. Neither of us has any self-control where the other's concerned. We know that by now."

He sighed. "I guess we do. What have you done to me, witch? How have you made me want things I never cared about before?"

"What things? Tell me about them."

"No, you know too much already. Maybe I'll let you find out gradually."

Still moving carefully, he laid his lips against her bruise. "Does that hurt?" he murmured.

"Not a bit," she said blissfully.

He continued, tracing a soft pattern down the side of her face. Debbie was already in heaven. Even if she had been in any pain it would all have been swallowed up in the joy of being in Jake's arms. All she was conscious of was happiness and the approach of indescribable pleasure.

But although she could forget her injury, *he* couldn't. Their previous lovemaking had been forceful and vigorous on both sides, half loving, half fighting, with no quarter asked or given: the way they both liked it. But now he loved her with a gentleness that brought tears to her eyes. His touch was feather-light, making not only her body but also her heart sing. There was no trace now of the harsh, sarcastic man she'd known. He was banished, and in his place was the most considerate lover a woman could have asked for.

She caressed him with delight, full of wonder that this big, male body could be so subtle, so loving. He was hard and lean under her roving hands, his power leashed back, his vigor restrained. Occasionally he smiled when she did something that especially pleased him. He had a wonderful smile, she thought, mysterious and full of depths for her to explore. One day.

"I dreamed that it could be like this," she whispered. "But I thought it could never be more than a dream."

"Some dreams can come true," he murmured. "What are you dreaming now?"

"Of you. Only of you—" She broke off with a gasp as his tongue teased first one nipple and then the other. At the same time she could feel him caressing the inside of her thighs with light, almost tickling movements that excited her. "I want you, Jake," she said softly.

He eased himself between her legs and entered her easily. "Tell me to stop if this is too much for you," he insisted.

She smiled in languorous delight. "Could you manage to stop?" she teased.

"If I have to. You'd be surprised what I can do if I have to."

But she wouldn't be surprised, she realized. This man could do anything. He was as strong as all the world, and as tender as a baby. And he was hers. He *must* be hers.

Her body relaxed under his gentle loving. Pleasure and happiness streamed through her. She tried to show her feelings through her movements and the language of her eyes. His own eyes were full of concern as they looked into hers, but was it only concern, she wondered? Did it amount to love, or was that no more than wishful thinking? Could any man hold a woman with such tenderness and not love her a little?

As she felt her moment approach Debbie wrapped both arms about his neck and let the world dissolve around her, leaving her floating in a new universe. It contained only Jake and herself, the feelings that united them, and all the feelings yet to come. She was being granted a glimpse of that bright future, and the joy of it made her cry out softly.

"Are you all right?" he asked as he eased himself away from her.

"I'm fine. Don't go."

He drew her close to him so that her head rested against his shoulder. "Come here," he murmured. "Let me hold you."

She lay against him, listening to the gradually slowing thunder of her own heart, wishing she could hear his heart, too, and know for sure that it was beating in time with hers. After a while languor overtook her and she fell asleep again, so she never saw the look on his face as he turned to her. It would have answered her question.

Once they'd opened the first doors to the discovery of each other, everything seemed to fall easily into place. It was sweet and natural to Debbie to lie naked with him, stretched across the bed, her head in his lap, telling him about herself.

"You?" he cried hilariously. "The daughter of academics?"

"Incredible, isn't it?" she agreed, joining in his laughter. "My father specializes in Medieval German literature, and he knows more about trolls and hobgoblins than about modern life. I'm sure he thought a troll must have spirited away their real daughter and left me in exchange. Luckily I've got a brother, Simon, who's everything I'm not, studious, serious, academic, all that stuff."

He regarded her cynically. "So you were lousy at school, huh?"

"Well, I passed the exams. Only just, sometimes, but I did pass. Dad was always convinced that I could do him proud if only I'd spend a little less time on the sports field and a little more time studying, but basically I couldn't see the point. Now, doing a lap of the running track faster than anyone else, there was point to that. And dancing. I used to wow them in the school concert. But book learning . . ." She wrinkled her nose. "I remember Simon telling my parents, 'It's a waste of time trying to turn Debbie into a swot. Her brains—such as they are—are of the kind known as shrewdness and low cunning.'"

"A perceptive young man" Jake observed with feeling.

"Definitely." Debbie chuckled. "Mind you, he got out of kicking range before he said it. But even I could see that he was right. When he said 'low cunning,' I recognized myself right off. No brains but plenty of savvy." She looked up at him indignantly. "Oy!"

"What?"

"When I said 'no brains' you were supposed to say something complimentary."

He kissed her. "I adore your savvy. Go on with the story. Was it low cunning that decided you on a career in the police?"

"No, that was later. I was going to be a dancer first. I joined a third-rate dancing act touring fourth-rate clubs. I thought it was so exciting to be independent. But when independence became simply a matter of peeling dressing rooms and never enough to eat, I found it wasn't exciting at all. So I went home and applied to join the police."

"What about your promotion exams? You passed them reasonably well."

"Been checking up on me, huh?"

"Of course."

"I did it with black coffee, sleepless nights and sheer slog. As soon as they were over I heaved a sigh of relief and forgot most of it."

Jake grinned. "Join the club."

She gave a reminiscent chuckle. "Chief Manners once complained that the reason I never did anything by the book was because I'd never bothered to read it. Actually I thought that was rather unjust."

"Well, you should forgive a man who's just had to rescue his newest detective sergeant from incarceration by a rival force, whose patch she'd invaded."

"You *have* been checking up on me." She kissed him thoroughly and announced, "I'm starving. Pizza all right?"

"Fine."

She microwaved a frozen pizza and they ate it with their fingers, washed down with a bottle of wine. Afterward they loved again before falling asleep. Jake slept first, and Debbie lay watching him, awed by the joy that had transformed her life and wondering how she'd ever endured life without it.

Jake awoke to find himself lying on his back, Debbie propped up on one elbow beside him. "All right," she said playfully. "Who is she?"

"Who's who?"

"My rival. The woman you talk about in your sleep."

"You don't have a rival."

"Then who's Patsy?"

The smile died out of his face, leaving it blank. She had the feeling of having run into a brick wall, and it hurt. "Hey," she said, trying to keep up the playful tone. "I was only kidding. I'm not the jealous type. She's probably your dog."

"No, she's not a dog." He fell silent, brooding darkly.

"All right, I shouldn't have asked," Debbie said. She minded badly, but she wasn't going to let him see.

"No, I ought to tell you. It might help you understand why I'm such a cantankerous so-and-so."

"You mean there's a reason?" she asked. "I thought you were just born that way."

He gave a brief smile. "Part of me was, I guess. And part of me got that way through working at it."

"And part of it was due to Patsy?" Debbie was holding her breath.

"Policewoman Patsy Selkirk," he said softly. "She was the best, the very best."

"The best what?"

"The best undercover cop I ever knew. We worked together on and off for years. There was nothing she was afraid of, nothing she wouldn't do."

There was a note in his voice that Debbie hadn't heard before. She lay quietly, hoping that he couldn't hear her heart, which had suddenly started to beat louder. She, too, prided herself on never being afraid, but she was afraid now, not of danger but of an indefinable something in Jake's manner when he spoke of Patsy Selkirk. His face bore a look of nostalgic melancholy as though his surroundings had vanished, leaving him with the echo of a dream in which Debbie had no part. And that scared her more than anything.

"You say you worked together," she ventured. "I thought you didn't like working with women."

"Not now I don't. In those days I accepted the new thinking. You had to treat female colleagues the same as men, expect them to be able to do the same—so I did." His voice became iron. "And because I did, Patsy Selkirk is lying six feet underneath a headstone with In Loving Memory engraved on it."

"Oh, my God! What happened?"

"Some cheap little bastard gunned her down without a second's thought. I should have been there with her. I might have stopped it. But I was around the other side of the building. 'Go on,' she said. 'You go and check it out. I'll be all right on my own.' So I took her word for it—that's what you're supposed to do these days. I heard the shots—ran back as fast as I could, but it was too late. She was dead."

"Did you get the man who did it?"

Jake spoke very quietly. "Oh, yes. I got him."

He didn't say any more. There was no need. But again he seemed to be looking into the past, only this time it was a dreadful past, in which he'd done terrible things, because they'd had to be done.

Debbie reached out and touched him. "Was that when you began to dislike working with women?" she asked.

"Of course. She was supposed to be there helping me. She assured me she wouldn't let me down. And what was she doing when I needed her? Lying dead. How unprofessional can you get?"

Debbie wasn't fooled by his tone. Jake was torn apart by this death, and savage irony was his way of coping. But was his pain due solely to self-blame, or something more? She hesitated a long time before asking her next question. She dreaded the answer. "Were you in love with her?" she asked softly.

He hesitated. "No—yes—perhaps. I don't know what people mean when they say that. I only know that her death hurt horribly, and feeling that I was to blame made it worse. I've played it safe by avoiding women ever since."

She regarded him with a little frown. "Did you mean that—about not knowing what love meant?"

This time he hesitated even longer. "I think it means something different to everyone. I've never really known what it could mean to me, where it could fit in my life. Patsy and I—" He stopped, and it seemed to Debbie that he was struggling on the edge of a revelation that scared him.

"You were lovers?" she prompted.

"Yes. But there was something else. If I'd only—"

Watching his face closely Debbie saw his inner struggle and the moment when he backed away. At last he let out a slow breath, and she knew he'd decided to keep his secret to himself. It didn't matter, she told herself to cover the hurt. They would have years to learn each other's secrets.

"I've never said the words," Jake said at last. He took a deep breath, wondering if his next confession would finish him in her eyes. But whatever he feared, the compulsion to be honest drove him on. "I wonder if I ever will say them—" he looked at her steadily "—even if they're true."

To his intense surprise she didn't react, but lay looking into space as though she were considering something beyond him. At last she murmured, "Well, they're only words, aren't they? And if you know the truth, you don't need words, as well."

"Do you mean that?" he asked intently.

"I grew up in a home where words were treated as if they were almost the only thing that mattered. I suppose it's made me a bit rebellious about them. While they were listening to the words, I was listening to the silences."

"Is that what you're doing now?" he ventured. He was holding his breath, wondering if he'd really stumbled on the one woman able to understand his awkwardness, or rather to look beyond it.

She smiled at him. "Some people's silences are more interesting than others."

There was a hint of teasing in her manner, and it had the effect of breaking the spell. Yet he had the feeling that she'd done it on purpose, knowing that neither of them was ready for too much intensity just yet.

They dozed again, and when they awoke it was dark. Jake realized that twenty-four hours had passed since he'd arrived. Between sleeping and loving they'd made their own night and day, letting the universe whirl on without them.

Debbie got to her feet and stretched. Jake watched her walk across the room, naked, beautiful, moving with the sensual relaxation of a woman at ease with her own body. And suddenly he was swept by an emotion he hadn't felt since his callow youth— jealousy. It was so unexpected and shocking that for a moment it held him dumb.

But if maturity had taught him anything it was when to play it cool. Instinct warned that nothing would scare off this independent lady quicker than a show of possessiveness. Leaning back, one arm behind his head, he surveyed her with a show of indifference and said casually, "I've told you my big secret. Don't I get to hear yours?"

She looked back, twisting her body so that shadows danced across its mounds and valleys in a way that sent riplets of delight scurrying through him. "Have I been talking in my sleep, too?" she chuckled.

"You mutter sometimes, but I haven't really been listening," he said untruthfully. "The only thing I heard clearly was 'Henry the Eighth.'"

"Henry the Eighth?" she echoed blankly. "Why on earth would I…" Her brow cleared. "Oh, yes, of course."

"You seem to be having a fling with a monarch who's been dead for four hundred years," he said. "I guess I can live with that."

"As a matter of fact, I am. In a way."

"In what way?" he asked with misgiving.

"Lucky. Henry the Eighth."

"You've lost me."

"Ever since I met Lucky I've been trying to think who he reminded me of. And suddenly it came to me. King Henry the Eighth."

"*Lucky*—"

"When Henry was courting Anne Boleyn. He was the king, and used to having everything his own way. Opposing him was the quickest way to get yourself wiped out."

"Like Lucky."

"Exactly. Anne was one of his subjects. He could simply have forced her. Instead he begged and pleaded. Listen." She reached into a small cupboard, took out a book and flicked through the pages until she came to the place she wanted. "This is one of his letters to her. 'I have never committed any offence against you, and it seems to me a very small return for the great love I bear you, to be kept at a distance from the person and presence of the one woman I most esteem in the world.'

"And in another letter he signs himself, 'Your loyal and most assured servant.'"

"So?"

"So, in his own way, Henry was a romantic, just like Lucky. He loved playing the servant to his cruel lady, but it was only a game. Anne kept Henry dangling for six years before he made it as far as her bed."

"How come you've got all this at your fingertips?" Jake demanded. "This is book learning, which you claim to know nothing about."

"I *do* know nothing about it," she defended herself indignantly. "It's not my fault that I come from learned stock. This book was written by my mother. Naturally I have to have a copy. I put it in a prominent place whenever she visits."

But he wasn't appeased. "You knew just where to turn in it," he accused. "You've read it."

"I haven't actually read it," she equivocated. "Not as in really 'read' it. But naturally I had to read it so that she wouldn't suspect I hadn't read it. It seems perfectly simple to me."

"If you say so. But I still feel deceived. You swore you were as ignorant as me."

"I *am* as ignorant as you," she asserted. "Almost."

He grinned as he pulled her down on the bed beside him and she snuggled up, still holding the book. "As I recall, Anne Boleyn came to a bad end," he said. "Once they were married he got bored, dropped all that servant and lady stuff, and had her beheaded on a trumped-up charge."

"Now who's been reading books?" she demanded accusingly.

"I did it at school," he protested. "Some of it stuck."

"How come? I pictured you getting through school by indulging fantasies about duffing up your opponents on the football field."

"You can't do that all the time," he explained reasonably. "When you're in class you have to pay some sort of attention so that the teachers don't suspect you're not paying attention. It seems perfectly simple to me." He took the book from her and examined the spine that bore the legend *Henry the Eighth* by Elspeth Harker.

"So your mother wrote this, huh? And your father specializes in Medieval German literature? I suppose he writes books, too?"

"Published by a specialist University Press," Debbie confirmed gloomily.

"And your brother?"

"The press has just taken his first book and an option for three more," she said with a sigh.

"Learned stock, indeed. I wonder how they'll feel about having me in the family."

The last words were little more than a mutter and Debbie barely heard them. She glanced up at him, eyebrows raised, but he seemed absorbed in the book and didn't meet her gaze.

They threw together a snack, consisting of whatever was easiest to cook, and ate it like children having a midnight feast. Then they got into the shower together and he soaped her down, careful to keep himself between her and the tiled wall. Afterward he dried her and carried her to bed and they enjoyed another kind of feast before falling into satiated sleep.

At some point in the early hours of the morning, half sleeping, half waking, Jake reached a conclusion about Debbie and about himself, about the two of them. Or rather, a conclusion was reached somewhere inside him, midway between his heart and his brain. It was less a conscious decision than a clearing of confusion and a recognition of the inevitable. When he awoke properly it was midmorning, and everything was very simple.

"There's something I want to tell you," he said.

But Debbie interrupted him with a hand over his mouth. "No words, Stoneface. We don't need them."

"Are you sure we don't need them, occasionally?" he asked, a touch wistfully.

"Let's put it this way. I don't want you to say anything that you have to force yourself to say. That's more dangerous than saying nothing. There are things I'm happy to take on trust."

"Well, I'm not," he said with sudden resolution. "Some words are better spoken, and I l—" The shrill of his mobile phone interrupted them. With a sign to Debbie to keep quiet, he answered it.

"Jake, is that you?" Debbie could just hear Lucky's tinny voice.

"Yes, Mr. Driver."

"Where the hell are you? Brian drove past earlier to-day and couldn't see you. Have you deserted your post?"

Jake improvised quickly. "I'm just inside the building, Mr. Driver. I've tucked myself into a corner of the hall downstairs. Nobody can see me but if Silver leaves I'll be bound to see her, and I can follow her." He mopped his brow.

"And *has* she left?"

"No, Mr. Driver."

"Not once?"

"Not once."

"Has anyone been to see her?"

"Not a soul."

Lucky's voice was iron-hard with suspicion. "Are you telling me that she's just stayed there all this time, doing nothing? C'mon, she's fooled you. She's got out when you weren't looking."

Suddenly inspired, Debbie went into a theatrical pan-tomime of sobbing. Jake twigged at once and his eyes met hers in the understanding of a perfect team. "I think she's very upset," he told Lucky. "I went to listen outside the door of her flat, and I'm sure I heard her crying."

"That's fine," Lucky purred. "That's just fine. Did she hear you?"

"No, she has no idea I'm around," Jake assured him.

Debbie gave a silent chuckle. Inspiration had come to her. Lucky had two telephones on his desk, with differ-ent lines. She knew which one he used most, and he was probably using it now to call Jake. She lifted her bed-room phone and began to dial the other.

As she dialed she was listening intently to Lucky's tinny voice coming through Jake's mobile. "Now, look, Blair, this is what I want you to do. Wait until—hang on, my other phone's ringing.'' He snatched up the other receiver. "Yes? Who's there?"

"It's me, Lucky," Debbie said in a whisper that was half a sob. Jake turned aghast eyes on her, but she only winked at him. "Are you still mad at me?"

"What do you think?" Now that she could hear him more clearly she could tell he'd been drinking.

"I think you're mad at me," she said sorrowfully. "Maybe you're right to be. I was a bad girl, wasn't I?"

"You can say that again."

"But I didn't mean to be, Lucky. I wanted to please you, but I guess I got it wrong. I don't suppose you'll ever forgive me, will you?"

"Hey, c'mon, I didn't say that. Everyone makes mistakes, okay?"

"Oh, Lucky, you're so sweet and generous."

"Wait a minute, sweetheart." His voice became muffled, so Debbie guessed he'd put a hand over the receiver, but she could hear him through Jake's phone. "Jake, are you there?"

"I'm here, Mr. Driver."

"Are you outside her door?"

Madness seized Debbie. Before Jake could answer she leaned over and brushed her lips against his. Before she could do it again he seized her firmly, keeping her at a distance. "I'm right there, Mr. Driver."

"Good. Can you hear what she's doing inside?"

Debbie hid an explosion of laughter against Jake's chest.

"Er, what she's doing?" Jake prevaricated. His forehead was damp. "You want to know what she's doing."

"Yes. What's the matter with you?"

"Nothing, Mr. Driver. Absolutely nothing. Just trying to concentrate on my job."

"Trying to? Why, is it hard?"

"It is sometimes," Jake admitted.

"Can you hear her through that door?"

"Yes, I can. She's talking, but I can't hear anyone else, so I think she's on the phone."

Lucky chuckled. "That's right, she's on the phone. Jake, I have to admit I doubted you. I wondered if you were really there. But if you know Silver's on the phone then you must be where you say you are. I should have trusted you, right?"

"You should have trusted me, Mr. Driver," Jake said in a hollow voice.

"Do you know who she's talking to? Me, Jake, me. That's right. She called up to make it up with me. Because—shall I tell you a secret?—if you show a woman who's boss, she loves it. Did you know that?"

"I didn't know that, Mr. Driver."

"She's been sitting by that phone waiting for me to call and say I was sorry, but I didn't call. So now she's called me, to beg my forgiveness. And that's the way it should be."

"Congratulations, Mr. Driver."

"So I'll let her tell me how sorry she is, and then maybe I'll forgive her, but I'll make her wait. That's the way to treat a woman, Jake."

"I'm sure you're right, Mr. Driver."

"You've got to keep them in their place. Don't ever let them think they can get the better of you."

Jake's gaze was fixed on Debbie, doubled up with silent laughter. His mouth was dry. "I'll remember that, Mr. Driver," he managed to say.

Lucky hung up without saying more. The next moment Debbie heard him on her own receiver. "Now, sweetheart, where were we?"

"I was saying what a wonderful, generous man you are, Lucky," she cooed.

"Well, I guess it's not hard to be generous to you," Lucky said thickly. Debbie heard a slight glugging sound as if he was still drinking heavily. "You really hurt me, Silver," he said sentimentally.

"I didn't mean to, Lucky. Besides, you hurt me, too, with some of those nasty things you said."

"When you come back I'll make it up to you, sweetie. You'll have anything you want, you just name it."

"Anything?" Debbie cooed, winking at Jake.

"Anything at all. Just to show how sorry I am for being mean to you. Ah, Silver, I've had a rotten few days worrying about you, wondering what you thought of me. I guess life wouldn't be worth living if I lost you."

Jake, his head close to the receiver, listened to these effusions with disgust. So Lucky believed in keeping a woman in her place, did he? And the minute this clever siren got working on him, he collapsed to jelly.

"Say you forgive me," Lucky pleaded.

"I forgive you, Lucky," she said sweetly.

"Can I come and see you?"

"No" she said quickly. "I'll see you this evening."

"Early this evening?"

"My usual time."

"I'll count the moments until then." Debbie heard him blowing a kiss.

She blew one back. "Until then. 'Bye, Lucky." Debbie replaced the receiver, then lay back on the bed and crowed with merriment. "Oh, Lord, what a prat he is!" she crowed. "I really enjoyed that."

"Yes, you did, didn't you?" Jake said quietly.

"Now, you have to admit I'm good at what I do," she teased him. "Did I bring him to heel or did I bring him to heel?"

"You brought him to heel," Jake agreed.

"Oh, let's forget about Lucky. Come here, lover. Hey, what are you doing?" Jake had risen and was pulling on his clothes.

"I have to get back to work."

"He's not expecting you back yet."

"No, but he's capable of coming by, despite your prohibition. You've done such a terrific job in making him your slave that there's no knowing how far he'll go. If he turns up, I mustn't be here."

It sounded reasonable enough, but Debbie had a horrible awareness of something wrong. Jake's voice had changed, grown distant, and he wasn't looking at her anymore. "Jake, what is it?" she asked quickly. "What's the matter?"

"Nothing's the matter. We had a holiday and now it's over and I must get back to work. It's safer that way."

"To hell with safer," she said furiously. "I want the real reason."

He hesitated. "I can't tell you."

"Whyever not?"

"Because I don't know how to put it into words," he said violently. "There are times when knowing how to say things would be useful. Now I have to go."

He walked out of her apartment, his body still pervaded by the passionate, whole-hearted abandon of her loving, hating himself for the ungenerous spirit that had made him turn away from her. But despite his scorn for himself, he couldn't help it.

Since her triumphant phone call, in which she'd reduced Lucky to a suppliant again within seconds, she looked different, a woman whose business was making fools of men. He tried to shake off the impression, to see again the bright, beautiful comrade and lover of his dreams, but it was no use. He'd been on the verge of telling her that he loved her, but he couldn't speak of love now. The words were ashes in his mouth.

And there was another feeling, one he couldn't place at first, but which he finally identified with a sense of incredulity. It was relief. The feelings that she'd aroused in him over the last few days had been of a depth and tenderness that alarmed him. They took him into new territory, where he wasn't sure he was ready to go.

But now it was all right. She wasn't perfect, after all. He was safe again.

Eight

Debbie's return was triumphant. Lucky filled her dressing room with white roses and showered her with luxurious gifts. The sight of her bruised forehead reduced him to stammering remorse, as though he were personally responsible for her slipping in her own shower. He declared over and over that he could never forgive himself for misjudging her, until she had to smother her boredom.

Her stock had never been higher. Everyone in the club knew about the quarrel and its cause, and had assumed she was finished. When it became clear that Lucky was more her slave than ever even Brian began to treat her with nervous respect. Jake treated her no way at all. He just quietly kept his distance.

After her first unhappy dismay Debbie called up her pride. Whatever was bugging him, she'd find out at last. In the meantime she refused to let him think his attitude was getting to her.

On her third evening back she sat in silence during the journey home, but when they reached her flat she silently indicated for him to get out and talk. "I've got news for you," she said when they were standing just outside her door. "Lucky's planning a big weekend party at his home. He's mending his fences with Rox Leverham and Dan Sedgewick. Remember them?"

"He neglected them to spend time with you."

"Right. But it's not just them. His telephone's been red-hot with people calling to accept and he doesn't send me away now when he's talking. This is more than a social weekend. It's also a kind of business conference. Things are going to be planned. And I'm coming to realize that Lucky isn't Mr. Big in this gathering. He acts like it, but today I heard him talking to someone he called 'sir.' He was practically in tears of gratitude because 'sir' was consenting to accept his hospitality."

"Have you any idea who this is?" Jake asked.

"No, but he's going to be there, this weekend."

"It makes sense," Jake mused. "Lucky's shrewd and cunning, but he's limited."

Debbie nodded. "He doesn't have the kind of real brains he'd need if he was running everything," she agreed. "But he's flashy and he enjoys the spotlight, so he's probably a useful front man for whoever's behind it. Anyway, we'll discover who it is over the weekend."

"You're going to be there?"

"I'm the hostess. Lucky's putting an understudy in the cabaret for a couple of nights. I'm going down alone on Friday morning. You'll follow on with Lucky and some of his more important guests. Lucky's lending me one of his lovely cars to drive." She sighed. "I think I might marry Lucky for the sake of his cars."

Once Jake would have reminded her that he, too, had a car that had made her eyes light up, and they would have laughed together. But tonight he didn't take the bait. Instead he nodded her a good-night and walked away, leaving her puzzled and with an aching heart.

Lucky's mansion was just outside London in the "stockbroker belt." Debbie arrived on Friday morning and found that the numerous servants had been briefed to expect her and follow her orders. Not that there was much to order. Everything was already organized and it was clear that she had only to put the finishing touches and parade around looking beautiful.

The house was in the style known as mock Tudor, but everything about it was mock, not just the dark beams, cunningly antiqued to look four hundred years old, or the leaded windows whose surrounds were actually made of the latest imperishable materials done up to look like wood. The whole soul of the place, insofar as it had a soul, was fake.

Much of the basement had been scooped out to make an indoor swimming pool, complete with Jacuzzi and sauna. Not content with this, Lucky, apparently feeling that wealth only counted if it was on display, had had another pool built on the grounds.

As she inspected the guest list and went over the house the cleverness of Lucky's plan became clear to her. Some of the guests were his criminal associates, who would stay overnight. Others were local bigwigs, invited to attend parties and barbecues. Lucky knew that the police were watching him, but at this party a surveillance patrol could sit and count the arrivals until their eyes crossed and they would learn almost nothing. The "real" guests would be lost in the camouflage.

Many of the permanent guests seemed to be unaccompanied men, and Debbie supposed it was for their benefit that a contingent of young ladies had been drafted in. They were to live in some trailers parked out of sight among some trees, and were obviously expected to be on call at all hours. To her dismay Debbie found a scribbled note from Lucky in the margin, indicating that as hostess it was her job to keep a supervisory eye on them.

"Didn't have the nerve to tell me to my face, huh?" she muttered crossly. "Are *all* men cowards? Well, there's no knowing where this job will lead. Just don't let anyone dare to call me Madam!"

Upstairs she found twenty guest bedrooms in addition to the palatial master bedroom that was Lucky's, with the connecting door to her own elegant boudoir, which was already decked with flowers. A huge bouquet of orchids lay in the center of the satin counterpane. Wrapped around the middle stem was a diamond bracelet with a note that said, "How long must I wait? Lucky."

Through the window she saw a man making his way up the front drive. He was small, elderly, and looked tired. She hurried down to greet him. "Is this Mr. Driver's residence?" he asked, regarding her benignly through pebble glasses.

"That's right."

"He invited me for the weekend. It looks very quiet. Am I the first to arrive? Oh, dear, what a terrible thing to do."

He looked so distressed that Debbie hastened to reassure him. "I'm not at all put out," she said warmly. "Why don't we have a drink, and then I'll show you to your room, Mr.—"

"Mr. Simpson. That's very kind of you, indeed. If I might have a little chamomile tea."

"Don't you want anything stronger than that? You look so tired. How do you come to be on foot?"

"I walked from the railway station."

"But it's nearly three miles."

"I just missed the last taxi. I thought I would get it but a young man dashed in front of me at the last minute. When I ventured to remonstrate, in the mildest terms, he called me a name I couldn't repeat to a lady. Please, don't worry if you haven't any chamomile tea. I always bring my own." He produced a box of sachets. "I'm sorry to be a nuisance but I'm afraid I suffer from an upset stomach, so it seems safer to take precautions."

As she put the kettle on, she asked, "Do you live near here, Mr. Simpson?"

"Oh, no, I come from the midlands. I'm a chemist, retired now."

"How do you come to know Lucky?"

"I knew his father. We've stayed in touch. He's always been very kind to me."

Debbie was surprised at this new insight into Lucky's character, but only briefly. His strain of tenderheartedness sat oddly with other aspects of his nature, but she knew better than anyone that it was there.

When she escorted Mr. Simpson upstairs she found, to her dismay, that he'd been allocated the smallest, least imposing bedroom. But Mr. Simpson was delighted, apparently unaware that he was being treated like a poor relation. "It's so nice and quiet up here," he assured her. "I shall have everything I want."

Lucky arrived later in the afternoon and swept into the house, trailing his guests behind him. Debbie played her part skillfully, but as soon as possible she got him alone. "Mr. Simpson walked in a while ago," she told him.

Lucky stared. "He walked?"

"Apparently someone jumped him for the last taxi at the station. Poor little man. He looks like the kind of person who always gets pushed aside."

Lucky grinned. "Yes, he does, doesn't he? Did you give him his chamomile tea?"

"Yes, and he was very pleased."

"I'll go and see him. Why are you looking at me like that?"

"I think it's just so nice of you to take care of him."

He grinned and put his arms around her. "Well, I'm a nice guy. Didn't anyone ever tell you?" He kissed the end of her nose.

"I don't think anyone mentioned it," she teased. "Tell me about it."

"Later. First I must go and see Mr. Simpson."

"Before you do, can't we find somewhere better for him than that little attic?"

"The room's fine, sweetie."

"No, it isn't. I'd like to swap him with Mr. Rivers in Room 15."

To her astonishment Lucky went deadly pale. "Change him with Rivers?" he echoed.

"I'm sure Mr. Rivers wouldn't mind."

Lucky seized her shoulders. "Have you done anything about this?"

"No, but—"

"Thank heavens! Now listen, sweetie, you drop this idea and never mention it again. That's an order."

"I'm sorry. Is it important that Rivers has that particular room?"

Lucky clutched his hair. "Rivers is—never mind. Just do as I say."

"All right. I'd better come and start acting like a hostess to the guests you brought with you."

"Not just yet. We've got things to talk about. I shan't need you until the rest of the guests get here in about an hour." He went to the door. "And remember what I said, no changing the rooms about." He hurried away.

"What's up with Lucky?" Jake asked, coming in a moment later. "He was out of here like a bat out of hell."

"I just wanted to change over a couple of the guest rooms," Debbie said. "When I suggested moving Rivers, he went crazy."

"Could Rivers be the brains, the one Lucky's afraid of?" Jake mused.

"He certainly looked alarmed at the thought of offending him just now."

"We'll have to bear it in mind."

He turned to go, but Debbie stopped him with a hand on his arm. "Not yet," she said. "There are things we have to get settled first."

"Another time," he said hurriedly. "We mustn't be seen talking together."

She shrugged. "If anybody sees us I'm complaining that one of my boxes got left behind, and I'm sure it was all your fault."

He looked at her bleakly, and she noticed with dismay that the hot antagonism she'd once seen in his eyes, when he was craving for her, had been replaced by a cold hostility. "I'm sure you'll play your part to the full," he said with something that was almost a sneer.

"What's that supposed to mean?"

"It means that I'm not sure where acting ends and reality begins."

"You've lost me."

His eyes were hard. "You really enjoy making a clown out of Lucky, don't you?"

"Yes. Why not? I thought you did, too."

"It's incidental to the job in hand."

"Of course it is, but I don't do my job any the worse for enjoying it. So what?"

Jake knew that he should stop this conversation now before he gave away too much, but things that had been gnawing at him for the last few days were fighting their way to the surface. "Maybe it's your enjoyment that bothers me," he said grimly. "What else are you enjoying? Making a clown out of *me*? Or will that be left for when this is over, and I'll turn into a good joke for your friends."

She gasped. "I don't know what's got into you—"

"Perhaps it's the grandstand view I'm getting of your techniques."

"I've never made fun of you."

"I don't think that's strictly true, Debbie. When we started and you knew I was on edge for you and couldn't have you, you really got a kick out of that, didn't you?"

"Only because I was on edge too, and it cheered me up to know that I wasn't alone."

"Was that the only reason? Or did you feel you'd won when you got under Stoneface's skin?"

"Jake, whatever's happened? One minute everything was all right, and the next—" She stopped and drew in a sharp breath. "It was when I spoke to Lucky on the phone, wasn't it? There was something about that call..." She searched his face. "Just because I made a fool of him—that was it, wasn't it? But why?"

"Maybe because you did it so easily, so naturally. It's like breathing to you, isn't it? We're all fools in your eyes. Lucky, me—fools to be led by the neck just because you perform a few clever tricks."

Debbie's eyes glinted with temper. "That has to be the most unprofessional remark you've ever made."

"Unpro—"

"Lucky's a criminal. *I'm* part of your team. But because your male pride is offended by the sight of a woman making a man look an idiot, you've changed sides."

He colored, uncomfortably aware that she was getting near the nerve. "Don't talk rubbish!"

"It isn't rubbish. I see it all now. I'm a woman, and therefore the enemy. Your sympathy is with Lucky, *a fellow man.* It overrides your sense of professional obligation to me."

"I'm fulfilling my professional obligation," he snapped. "But it doesn't extend to your bed, and in future it won't. It's better for both of us that way. After all, you've got what you wanted."

"What the hell does that mean?"

"I know you by now, Debbie. You enjoy a challenge. I admire that, as long as I'm not the object. Stone face, stone heart, isn't that what Manners told you?"

"So what if he did?"

"So that's when you laid your plans."

She squared up to him. "I laid them much sooner than that, Jake. I laid my plans on the day we met. Because I liked you, I *wanted* you. But don't kid yourself that it was a challenge. Actually, you were very easy prey."

"Well, now the prey's slipped out of your grasp," he said, very pale.

"That wasn't what I—oh, go to the devil!"

"In my own good time," he said, and left her.

She stormed up to her room and dressed in a temper. She hadn't thought Jake could be so hard and unreasonable. Or so unperceptive as to confuse her treatment of Lucky with her treatment of himself. Masculine pride! she thought furiously. To hell with it! It was nothing but a device for spoiling what should be simple and straightforward.

But when her fury faded she found she was left with a strange ache, somewhere in the region of her heart, that had never been there before. It was half-true that she'd regarded Stoneface as a challenge to be won over. But only half-true. The call of like to like had been stronger than any feeling she'd known before in her life. She resisted the thought that she loved him, but she knew she *could* have loved him—if he hadn't turned out to be pigheaded and obstinate and too dense to see what was under his nose.

But he had turned out to be all these things, and fortunately she'd discovered in time. It was just that the ache in her heart wouldn't go away.

The guests were arriving in force now. Debbie went down to greet them, and her next few hours were taken up by being the perfect hostess. These were the "serious" guests, who would stay overnight. One or two of them had wives or other female company, but mostly they were alone. They included Rox Leverham and Dan Sedgewick, who both looked Debbie over as though trying to assess what she had that had made Lucky such poor company of late.

As it was a fiercely hot summer day a buffet meal was served around the pool. The young ladies emerged from their trailers and sauntered around in bikinis, serving drinks. Jake, also serving, looked up suddenly to see Debbie returning to the house. She reappeared a few minutes later, minus the sweater and slacks she'd been wearing earlier and clad only in a minute bikini. The few small triangles of material were gold lamé, held in place by delicate gold chains. Another gold chain encircled her waist, and high-heeled gold sandals adorned her feet.

Every man in the place watched, riveted, as she approached.

Almost every man. After the first glance Jake looked away. This was another of her tricks, rubbing his nose in it, forcing him to recognize that her erotic allure still worked on him, despite his antagonism. But she was mistaken. It was over. She couldn't affect him now.

"What d'ya think?" Lucky demanded, slapping him on the back. "Doesn't she put them all in the shade?"

"Miss Silver is always beautiful," Jake declared respectfully.

"Of course. But she doesn't always make the best of herself. I had to tell her to put that thing on. I don't like to see the other lovelies casting her in the shade. It makes me lose face. And that's something I can't afford."

"No, sir."

"She said she'd dressed plain so as not to offend me, after that little misunderstanding, y'know. But I told her to knock their eyes out. Everyone here knows she's mine." He smacked his lips. "Every inch mine," he repeated slowly. "Look at them, Jake. They all want her, and they know they can't have her. Ain't that the best feeling in the world?"

"I wouldn't know, sir."

Lucky chuckled. "I guess you wouldn't. Never mind. There are plenty of other lovelies around. There'll be one to spare for you."

"Thank you, sir." Jake spoke blankly to cover his inner turmoil. Lucky's revelation had altered the light, casting an ugly glow over the scene. He looked around at the men regarding Debbie with lustful eyes. He'd heard of most of them, knew their criminal records: extortion, assault, killing. They looked like respectable businessmen, but there wasn't one whose soul wasn't heavy with evil.

And the woman who'd touched his heart wandered among them, nearly naked. Not, as Jake had thought, because she was aiming a shaft at him, but because Lucky had ordered it. It was part of doing her job well.

Jake was used to danger, but he was also used to facing it with a gun. He had one on him now, concealed in his clothing. But she smiled and faced danger with no defense but her beauty, and sometimes that very beauty enhanced the danger. The men basking in her smiles would change from lust to cold brutality in an instant if they suspected the truth about her. And they would smash her without a second thought.

He tried not to think about another woman, who'd laughed and fought beside him, and ended up lying still with her laughter silenced forever. But the thought was there, and now he was sorry for the way he'd spoken to Debbie earlier. He wished he could get her alone to tell her that although he'd backed away from their personal relationship, he was right there with her where the job was concerned. But she was laughing at her admirers, and never once looked up.

As the sun went down people began to drift away from the pool to change their clothes for the evening party. More guests began to arrive for dinner. Debbie reappeared in an evening dress that, for her, was a model of decorum, and greeted dignitaries from the local chamber of commerce.

The first part of the evening followed fairly sedate lines. Debbie hosted a meal that was almost a banquet. It finished with toasts. Several men made speeches about Lucky's generosity to local good causes, while he smiled and looked modest.

Afterward there was dancing. Debbie found herself monopolized by a plump young man called Danvers, one of Lucky's associates. He had bad breath, made bad jokes and kept trying to see down her dress, while holding her much too close. She tried to get Lucky's attention but he was deep in conversation with one of his henchmen. As soon as the dance ended she steered him firmly off the floor. "Let's have another," he said, grinning stupidly.

"I'd love to, but I have to do my duty by everybody," she said, propping him against the bar.

"But—"

Before he could protest Debbie swooped on a man sitting at the bar sipping mineral water. "Mr. Simpson," she cried gaily, "I promised you a dance, didn't I?"

"Indeed you did," the little man said, reading the situation instantly. "I was about to come and claim it."

When they were on the floor she said, "Thank you for rescuing me. That was getting difficult."

He beamed. "I've never saved a damsel in distress before. What a splendid evening! But at my age, you know, jollity is a little exhausting. So if you'll forgive me, I'll retire when this dance is over."

She followed him into the hall and stood watching as he climbed the stairs. Then she swung around and cannoned straight into Danvers. "Not again," she said. "I have guests to see to."

"I'm a guest," Danvers insisted. He gave her a lecherous leer and blasted her with alcohol fumes. "You can see to me anytime you like."

He made a lunge and managed to get his arms about her. Debbie wriggled, twisting her head aside to escape the worst of his boozy breath. "Get—off—me," she said, fighting the temptation to blow her cover with a technique that would have sent him to sleep for the rest of the evening.

But he was beyond hearing her. There was nothing for it, she reckoned, but to play the Victorian maiden. Taking a deep breath she wailed, "Help—Lucky, help!"

There was a rush of feet, a confusion of raised voices, and the next moment Danvers had been felled to the floor by Lucky's fist. He hauled him up again at once and slapped him back and forth, his face a mask of vicious hate. "You're going to be sorry you did that—" Slap! "Nobody touches Silver—" Slap! "D'you understand that?" Slap!

Danvers was gibbering with fear, less from the blows than from something he saw in Lucky's face. Debbie didn't like Danvers but she couldn't stand by while he was murdered. She clutched Lucky's arm, speaking breathlessly. "Oh, Lucky, darling, I'm so glad you came to take care of me."

"Of course I take care of you, sweetheart. And now I'm going to take care of *him*."

"Let him go now," she pleaded. "I hate violence. It— it makes me feel faint." She swayed, forcing Lucky to catch her.

"Don't you worry your pretty little head about a thing," he murmured.

Ye gods! she thought. *He said it. He actually said, "Don't you worry your pretty little head." He deserves everything he gets.*

She fluttered her eyelids. "I'm not worried with you around, Lucky." She clutched him. "Don't go away."

"Jake."

"Sir?" Jake had been watching the little scene from well back but now he stepped forward.

"Take this lump of nothing outside and deal with him."

"You seem to have dealt with him pretty much already, boss."

Lucky's eyes were very cold. "I mean—*deal with him.*"

"Yes, boss."

Jake hauled the wretched Danvers outside. He knew quite well what he was expected to do, and Danvers knew it, too, because he was moaning softly. "Shut up!" Jake muttered.

A quick call on his mobile phone brought a car gliding silently to the entrance of the estate. Jake was waiting there, propping up Danvers who was regaining consciousness.

Manners put his head out of the car. "You said you'd got something for me."

"Here." Jake indicated Danvers. "He's one of Lucky's men and Lucky's just ordered me to kill him, so he'll probably be glad to talk."

Someone opened the rear door. As Danvers prepared to climb in, Jake's feelings finally got the better of him. Raising his foot he placed it firmly in the center of Danvers plump rear, sending him sprawling into the car.

"That was for *her,*" he said savagely. "And you're lucky it's all the law allows me."

Nine

"**D**anvers is dead. Jake's a reliable man. He even made the body vanish."

Debbie pressed close to the connecting door between her room and Lucky's, trying to hear everything he was saying into the phone. It was the next morning and she'd just stepped out of the shower when she'd heard Lucky on the telephone.

"The meeting's all set for tomorrow night, in the library," he was saying. "No—*tomorrow* night. What's that?—I said the same, but tomorrow is when he wants it. There's lot to be finalized."

She heard the receiver being replaced, then the sound of Lucky moving around. She dressed as quickly as she could and got out of the room, hoping to find Jake and tell him what she'd learned. He was just coming into the house as she reached the bottom of the stairs, but before she could speak she heard Lucky's voice above. "Hey,

Silver, I thought you'd wait and come downstairs with me."

She turned and said in a petulant voice, "Honey, I just have to have some new nail varnish. I've run out of my favorite color. Jake must run me into town."

But Lucky shook his head. "Sorry, sweetie, I haven't got a car available. Brian's fetching someone in the Rolls and the other car's out getting supplies. Whatever you wear you'll look beautiful. Besides..." He grinned significantly. "I don't think I'll notice your nail varnish."

She laughed and let him kiss her. When his head moved away she saw that Jake was still there, watching them, his face a blank. He was dressed in canvas shorts and a sleeveless olive green vest, and his skin was gleaming as if he'd been working hard.

"There are a dozen crates of champagne to be brought up from the cellar," she said. "I need Jake to do that."

"Sweetheart, he'll do whatever you want."

"Fine." Debbie beamed. "Now I'm going to have a nice, relaxing sauna."

Lucky slipped his arm about her waist and nuzzled her hair, murmuring, "That's right, darling. Be at your best for tonight, because it's going to be a special occasion."

Debbie's only answer to this was an idiotic giggle. She kissed Lucky on the nose and smiled coolly at Jake. "Well, you'd better get on with those crates, hadn't you?" she said before sauntering away.

She'd done her best, she reflected as she stripped off for the sauna and took a huge, luxurious white towel. Now it was up to Jake to take the hint. The heat hit her like a hot blanket as she stepped inside the wooden cabin. She tossed some pine-scented liquid onto the coals before lying down on one of the wide mattresses, covered by the towel, en-

joying the heat and thinking about Jake. How soon would
he find a way to join her?

The steamy atmosphere was affecting her, making her
heart beat slow and her blood pound strongly in her veins.
A light film of perspiration appeared all over her body.
She dabbed herself with the towel, thinking how sad it was
to be here naked, and no Jake to appreciate her.

At last there came the sound she was waiting for, a light
tap on the door. "Who's there?" she called sleepily.

"Jake."

"Come in. It's not locked."

He came in and locked the door behind him. "Did I
read you right?" he asked. "You wanted to talk to me?"

"Yes. What happened about Danvers? I heard Lucky
saying you'd disposed of him and even managed to make
the body disappear. But you couldn't have—"

"Of course not. The body is occupying a police cell
right this minute. You didn't really think—"

"No," she said quickly. "At least—I don't know you
anymore, Jake. How far would you go to keep your cover
intact?"

"About as far as you, I suppose," he observed distantly. Now, he thought, she would tell him what had
happened between her and Lucky the night before, and
put him out of his misery. Then he remembered that he'd
rejected her, and she owed him no explanations. But still
he hoped.

Debbie looked at him, daring him to ask the question
that she knew must be on his mind. But he stayed silent,
leaning against the wall and regarding her with a face that
revealed no sign of an inner struggle. "Stoneface," she
said softly.

"Stone face, stone heart," he agreed.

"I don't believe that, Jake."

"Believe it. It's true. Was this all you wanted me for?"

"No. I heard Lucky talking on the phone this morning. The big meeting is for tomorrow night, and it's going to be in the library."

"Then I've got to try to be in there. Or maybe you can manage it. If he trusts you enough to say all this in front of you—"

"He doesn't. I was listening behind the door between our rooms. He didn't know I was there."

He looked at her, trying to believe the implications. "He didn't know that you—?"

"I keep that door locked," she said simply. "All the time. And I stay on my side of it."

Joy rioted inside him, but he let none of it appear on his face. His brief relenting of the day before had been swept away by the sight of her lying there, regarding him with supreme confidence. She was so sure that she could make him her clown, he thought bitterly. And he'd so nearly let it happen again. He set his face in the familiar lines of stone.

Debbie was nettled by this apparent indifference. Just who did he think he was? He'd accused her of seducing him because of the challenge, and she'd denied it, but things were changing by the minute. Perhaps it was time she accepted that challenge and taught him a lesson. "Do you think I'm approaching the problem in the right way?" she asked demurely.

He gave her a shrewd look. "You're the best judge of how to keep Lucky on hot coals."

She chuckled. "Don't talk about hot coals in here," she advised.

"Good grief, what is this place?"

"It's a sauna. Haven't you ever been in one before?"

"No, thank God! I suppose it's one of those finer things of life that I'm too coarse to appreciate?"

"Well you obviously don't know how to dress in a sauna."

"What would be suitable? Top hat and tails?" he demanded ironically.

"Nothing. You're supposed to undress and let the heat get to you."

"I'm a hired hand. I'm not here for pleasure." Water was running down Jake's face. He mopped it with a handkerchief, then, finding this inadequate, he unthinkingly snatched at Debbie's towel, leaving her uncovered. He quickly replaced the towel, avoiding her eyes, which were full of mischief. "And you can cut out the games," he advised.

"I'm not playing games, Jake."

"Like hell. It wasn't just an accident that you happened to mention 'a nice, relaxing sauna' in front of me, was it?"

"I needed to talk to you in private and there was no other way."

"Well you've talked to me. Thank you for the information—"

"But I need more. I want your advice about how to deal with Lucky tonight. You heard what he was saying about a special occasion."

"You seem to have given him the green light," he snapped. Steam was coming off him, and Debbie guessed it wasn't just the sauna that was doing it.

"Keeping him at arm's length was wearing thin," she explained solemnly. "I had to change the record."

"I hope you know what you're doing."

Debbie propped herself up on one elbow, well aware that the angle caused the towel to fall away, revealing one breast. "Jake," she said, "who was it told me that nothing must be allowed to get in the way of the job?"

"*I did.*"

She reached up and touched him with her free hand, letting her fingers trail down his arm. She could feel him fighting not to respond. "Is any sacrifice too great to put this monster behind bars?" she murmured.

He turned bitter eyes on her. "What do you think?"

"Me? You're the leader in this campaign. I merely obey orders. What *are* your orders for tonight, Jake?"

He struggled to get the words out but they wouldn't come. He knew what the right answer was, but his professional detachment had deserted him. No power on earth could make him order her into another man's bed. The feeling of her fingertips tracing patterns on his arm was doing devastating things to him. He seized her hand to still it, but the magic remained. He looked at her through smoldering eyes. "Was that why you got me here?" he growled. "To ask my permission to sleep with him?"

"Well, no, perhaps that's one of those decisions that's best made in the field," she said thoughtfully. "Of course, letting him have what he wants might be a clever move. If he's unguarded when he's in a temper, imagine how loose his tongue might get—under certain circumstances. What a feather in my cap it will be to have helped put Lucky Driver in jail."

"And that's all that matters, isn't it?" he demanded bitterly. "The kudos, the step up in your career—"

"And *your* career, don't forget."

"To hell with my career," he said savagely. "I don't want you in his bed, do you understand?"

Her heart leapt, but she simply regarded him, wide-eyed. "I can't think why." She pouted.

"You know exactly why."

"No. At one time I'd have known why. But that's over, isn't it, Jake?"

"Yes," he growled.

"You think I'm a scheming, heartless minx who lured you on for the fun of it, and was planning to add your scalp to the others on her mantelpiece. So you decided— somewhat belatedly—to show me how strong-minded you were, and how easy you found it to resist me. You *do* find it easy to resist me, don't you, Jake?"

"Extremely," he snapped.

"So I needn't bother with this, need I?" With a swift movement she tossed the towel aside and lay looking up at him, as shameless in her glorious nakedness as a wood nymph.

He drew in a sharp breath. Their eyes locked in a silent battle of wills. Jake knew it had been madness to come in here and even greater madness to stay. The heat was pulverizing, making his whole body throb. He ought to get up right now and walk out, leaving temptation behind, and that was what he was going to do, any minute. But something seemed to hold him there, paralyzed. He couldn't take his eyes away from her, and as long as she held his gaze she had him trapped.

A light glow of perspiration covered her whole body as she lay there, her breasts rising and falling quickly. He knew that rapid motion. It happened when she was ready for love, and despite his brain's rejection, his heart and his senses persisted in finding it the most beautiful sight in the world.

His mind made a last desperate effort to protect him. *Beware her,* it whispered. *Don't give her the triumph of knowing she can jerk your leash and bring you to heel anytime she wants.*

But the voice of good sense faded beneath the onslaught of his craving for her. Reluctantly, unable to stop himself, he put out a hand and encompassed one beautiful breast. At once she gasped and arched upward, into his hand, responding with the speed and frankness that he loved about her.

No, not loved, he told himself. *You saw the danger and escaped in time. Remember? Remember...*

The voice faded into silence. He touched her other breast, adoring the way her face flushed in eager response.

"Take this off, Jake," she murmured, pulling at his vest.

He gasped and seized the towel to rub his face. Somehow, while he was thus occupied, she pulled the vest out of his shorts and had it halfway over his head. She ran her hands over his bare chest and the feel of it was so good that he almost groaned aloud. Her light touches set off scurries of delight that reached down over the skin of his torso, down into his loins. When she touched his belt he no longer had any power to resist her—if, indeed, he'd ever had it—but wrenched at the buckle himself.

"Is that what you want?" he growled.

"Yes," she said softly, surveying his nakedness. "That's exactly what I want. Come here, Jake."

Even without her urging no power on earth could have restrained him then. There were no more preliminaries. They were both already way beyond that point. As he lay down she parted her legs and he entered her instantly, explosively.

It was the best thing he'd ever known. She enclosed him fiercely in a hot darkness that sent waves of pleasure through his frame so forcefully that he wondered how he was holding together. He responded to her incitement by thrusting vigorously and was rewarded by the wild delight in her face. She was smiling at him— perhaps laughing— how could he know? An insane desire to discover what lay behind that smile drove him on to make her completely his again and again. As their moment came he experienced a dazzling sensation of being one with her, and she with him. For one brief second all the mysteries were solved, the questions answered, the puzzles made clear. She was as she'd appeared during those few days in her flat, the lover and comrade of his dreams, the woman he'd thought never to meet.

But it was an illusion. He might tell himself all these things while she lay beneath him, holding him eagerly, gasping with satiation. But the moment passed, try as he might to grasp it. She was a stranger again, and he could feel his own face hardening into lines of stone. Stone face, stone heart! If only it were true!

"Jake—" she said softly.

"I must go quickly," he growled. "This isn't safe."

"Jake—please . . ."

He refused to hear her pleading tone. A blinding anger was consuming him. She'd challenged him to resist her, and he'd failed. She'd made a fool of him yet again, that was all that had happened. Nothing else! Just that! It left a bitter taste in his mouth as he dressed hurriedly and left the sauna, pretending not to see the hurt look on her face.

The previous evening's party had been for the transient guests, including local worthies. Tonight's collection were rougher, more like Lucky's usual associates.

Debbie moved about like an automaton, while her mind went over and over the events of that morning. She was too shrewd not to know that she'd lost at the very moment of victory. By proving to Jake that she could bring him back to her arms whenever she liked, she had, para-doxically, driven him further off. He distrusted her allure even while he succumbed to it, and whatever his feelings for her might be, they plainly weren't strong enough to overcome that suspicion.

As the evening came to an end she knew that Lucky was regarding her with hot-eyed anticipation. She gave him her best inviting smile in return, but inwardly she was calculating just how drunk he was, and what she would have to do to make him pass out. "I feel like a real cele-bration," he said with meaning.

"So do I," she murmured back. "Let's celebrate with a Hot Lady, and then we can . . ." She let her eyes tell the rest of the tale.

A Hot Lady was a cocktail of her own devising. Lucky loved it, especially now. "A Hot Lady from a real hot lady," he growled.

She laughed and freed herself to head for the bar. The barman took out the drinks she commanded and then re-treated. As she mixed and shook she glanced at the glum figure sitting at the bar. "What are you doing here?" she asked. "Aren't you supposed to be on duty?"

"Mr. Driver said I could have the rest of the evening off to enjoy myself," Jake explained, tossing back his drink.

"You don't look as if you're having fun."

"I'm thinking about you going from me this morning to him tonight."

"A good operative does what the situation demands."

"Lady, you are using up your nine lives, very fast."

Debbie had placed her purse beneath the bar. Now she slid her hand in unobtrusively and took out a tiny vial, filled with something that would put Lucky in a very sound sleep for the rest of the night. Unnoticed, she emptied it into the cocktail shaker. It was easier to do this than put it in Lucky's glass alone, although it meant that her glass, too, contained the knockout drops. Somehow she would have to contrive to dispose of it, unseen. Lucky appeared just as she moved out from behind the bar to come in search of him.

"Hey, Jake, why so gloomy?" Lucky demanded. "It's a great night. A night for love." He took one of the cocktails Debbie was holding.

"Sure it is," Jake managed to say.

"I want to be good to all the world," Lucky said expansively. "Here, have one of Silver's 'specials.' She calls them Hot Ladies." He pressed his glass onto Jake. "Have a Hot Lady from a hot lady," he repeated, and laughed uproariously at his own joke.

Debbie drew in her breath at the sight of Jake about to swallow the spiked cocktail. Moving fast, she put the other glass in Lucky's hand and turned so that her arm struck Jake and the liquid spilled all over her.

"Clumsy idiot," she snapped. "Look what you've done to my dress!"

"Hey, I'll buy you another," Lucky said easily. "I'll buy you a dozen, a hundred."

"I apologize, ma'am," Jake said wryly.

Lucky sipped his drink. "Forget it, sweetie. You're not going to be wearing that dress much longer tonight anyway." He chuckled throatily and nuzzled her. "Jake, you know what's the trouble with you?"

"No, sir," Jake replied.

"I do," Debbie said petulantly. "He's congenitally clumsy."

"C'mon, sweetie, give him a break. No wonder you're looking so down, Jake. You need a little playmate. Hey Silver, who can we fix him up with?"

"Nobody," she said sharply. "He's got his duties to attend to."

"But you and I can't be the only ones to have fun tonight. I feel like being generous."

"I think you'll find that all the female company has been claimed," Debbie said coolly.

"Oh, I reckon I could entice one of those ladies to my side if I really tried," Jake said laconically. He was watching Debbie through narrowed eyelids. She met his gaze, hoping her inner disturbance didn't show. The thought of him with another woman— damn him! He was just doing this to make her suffer, because he was angry about Lucky.

Lucky drained his drink. "I'm ready to turn in," he said, winding his arm about Debbie's waist. "Want me to hijack one of those little popsies for you, Jake?"

"Nonsense, darling," Debbie said before Jake could answer. "You heard him. He's quite capable of hijacking a popsie for himself. Aren't you, Jake?"

"That's right, ma'am."

"In fact, I'm sure you think you can get any woman you set your heart on?" It was fortunate that Lucky was too vague by now to hear the edge on her voice.

Jake surveyed her, his head on one side. "My mind," he said quietly.

"What?"

"Set my *mind* on. I've never met the woman yet that I've set my heart on."

"Indeed," she responded coldly. "You must tell me the fascinating story of your love life some other time. Lucky, I want to go to bed."

"I've been wanting that for the past few hours, sweetie."

Arms entwined, they climbed the stairs together and entered Lucky's bedroom. As soon as he tried to undress her she said, ''No, let me do it. I want to strip for you, Lucky. I've really looked forward to that.''

She led him to the bed and arranged the pillows so that he could lean back and watch her. His eyes were already beginning to droop. Then she walked a few feet away, waited until she was certain she had his whole attention, and began to slither out of the dress with slow, sensuous movements. He regarded her openmouthed, fighting to stay awake, but it was a losing battle. By the time she was down to her underwear Lucky was out cold.

She undressed him, pulling his clothes off carefully, one by one, and tossing them into little crumpled piles on the floor, just as they might have fallen if he'd wrenched them off in a passion. In a spirit of pure mischief she ripped off a couple of buttons. When Lucky was naked she pulled the covers down on the free side of the bed, and rolled him over, draping a sheet across him. Then she went to settle herself comfortably on a large sofa by the window. She'd considered retiring to her own room but rejected the idea. If Lucky awoke in the night she needed to be in his room, as he expected.

It was a comfortable sofa and she was very tired, but for some reason she couldn't sleep. The thought of Jake was there to torment her. She was furious with him. What *she* had to do was for the sake of the job. What he did was entirely different.

In the early hours, when the world was still and quiet, she got up and went out onto the little balcony outside the window. There was a brilliant moon lighting up the landscape and casting the house and trees into deep shadow.

A faint rustling from the bushes below made her look down quickly. She almost thought she could see a man's form, but she couldn't be sure. She waited, holding her breath, watching the spot, but whoever was down there was also standing motionless.

Ten

___

Next morning Debbie was awake with the dawn. She uncurled herself from the sofa, stretching to get the kinks out of her limbs. A glance out of the window to the spot where a ghostly presence had stood the night before revealed that there was nobody there.

She took a wry look at Lucky's sleeping form. He was sprawled over most of the double bed, his mouth slack and gross, like a man satiated with physical love.

She collected her swimming gear from her own room, then crept down through the house to the underground pool. At this hour there was nobody else up and she enjoyed the freedom to swim alone in the cool water. She did length after length, relishing the physical exertion. When she turned for the last lap she could see Jake standing at the far end, waiting for her, his expression tense. With leisurely strokes she glided toward him. He kept his eyes on her until she was close, then nodded toward the side for her to come out of the water. The grimness of his face didn't relax.

"Good morning," she called cheerily, making no attempt to come out.

"I need to talk to you," he said bluntly.

"We'll talk when I've finished my swim," she announced, and began to backstroke away from him. She saw his face darken into a scowl, but kept swimming. Let him suffer!

As she started the return lap she saw that he'd stripped off and was climbing the ladder up to the high board. By the time she reached his end he was standing on the top board, arms folded, his face dark and brooding. When he ignored her wave she sank down into the depths. Looking up through the water she could discern the wavy outlines of the board and the man standing grimly on the top.

Then something darkened the light above, and the next moment the water was shaken as he dived right down beside her, swimming beneath and around, catching her up in turbulence. She twisted and writhed around him, staying just out of reach, laughing at him through the water and wriggling out of the way when he reached for her. Then she kicked her feet against the side of the pool and raced away to the far end. Taken by surprise, he gave her a head start and it took him the length of the pool to catch up. By the time they'd returned to the deep end he was in the lead, but only just.

She surfaced and pushed her hair back. "Nothing like a nice healthy swim in the morning," she said with dreadful heartiness.

"Yes, especially after an energetic night," he said morosely. "I trust it was worth it. You ought to get a diamond tiara for breakfast at least."

"And what about you? Lucky gave you the night off to make whoopee with Flossie or Zizi, or whoever took your fancy."

"It might have been Flossie *and* Zizi," he said coolly. "I was feeling energetic."

"Then it's a pity you wasted the night under Lucky's window," she said, laughing.

He ground his teeth. "Security is part of my job."

"Oh, Jake," she said softly, "you're a fool."

"I won't argue with that. I'm just not the kind of fool you took me for."

"I never took you for as big a fool as you're proving to be. Didn't you wonder why I knocked that Hot Lady out of your hand? I spiked that cocktail shaker with a heavy sleeping drug. If you'd drunk anything from it you wouldn't have been any use to Flossie *or* Zizi."

"And Lucky?" he asked, watching her intently.

"He had the other drink from the shaker. We just made it upstairs before he passed out. I undressed him and put him to bed, then I strewed our clothes around for artistic effect. He'll awake hoping he had the night of his life and wondering why he can't remember it." A sudden flash of temper made her add, "But I forgot, whenever I put one across on him you take his side and I look like Messalina, don't I?"

She dived back into the water before he could reply, leaving him a prey to mixed feelings. Would the time ever come, he wondered, when his feelings about her wouldn't be mixed?

He dived into the water after her, and when he glided down beside her she looked up at him enigmatically. While he was still trying to divine her meaning she took his face between her two hands and pulled it closer to her own. A stream of little bubbles floated to the surface as she laid her lips lingeringly over his. She intertwined her legs with his and moved her lips against his mouth, reminding him of kisses they'd shared, silently asking him how she could allow another man to touch her when she'd lain in *his* arms. But he was being painfully stupid about it. She would gladly have stayed there, explaining the matter to him all day, but she was fast running out of air. Suddenly she broke free from him and streamed up to the light, gasping as she reached the surface.

"Was that supposed to tell me anything?" he demanded. His tone was belligerent but he looked shaken.

"Oh, really!" she said, exasperated. "Work it out. Work it all out."

He followed her into the changing rooms and stood watching as she wrapped a robe around her. "I came to give you something," he said, feeling in his bag. "If I can't get into the meeting tonight we need a way of listening in." He handed her a small object. "It's a bug. You'll have to find a way of planting it in there."

"That shouldn't be any problem." She took the bug. "Now I'd better be getting back before Lucky misses me." At the door she turned and looked at him. "Jake, you did spend the *whole* night under my window, didn't you?"

"I may have done."

"You'd better have done." She hurried away, leaving him looking after her with a wry smile on his face.

On her way back to her bedroom Debbie paused outside Lucky's room. She could hear the sound of splashing from his bathroom, accompanied by loud, out-of-tune singing. Evidently Lucky felt he had something to be happy about.

Half an hour later, coolly dressed in a silk lemon top and brown canvas shorts, she went looking for him, and found him in the garden talking to Jake and Brian. She prepared to back away, thinking that if Jake was hearing anything interesting it was better to leave them to it, but Lucky looked up and saw her. "Hi, sweetheart," he said, stretching out an arm to her.

But his eyes were uncertain. Lucky didn't know what had happened the night before and he was hoping to learn it from her manner. Conscious of Jake's ironic gaze on her, she sauntered up, kissed Lucky briefly and murmured, "Hello, Tiger."

Lucky beamed.

Brian scowled.

Jake suppressed a grin.

"Your guests are beginning to come down to breakfast," Debbie said. "We'd better go in and be ready for them."

"I wish they'd all go to blazes and leave us alone," Lucky said.

"Oh, so do I, Tiger. Especially after—" Debbie broke off and giggled inanely.

"Sweetie," Lucky protested, "you're making me blush."

"Boss, it's going to be a busy day," Brian growled.

"Yes," Lucky agreed reluctantly. "Okay, let's go to breakfast." He began to make his way back to the house, Debbie's arm tucked in his.

"Boss," Brian called. "Before you see anyone, there are things to be talked about." He looked at Jake with jealous dislike. "Alone."

"Ah, yes. Now I remember." Lucky freed his arm. "I'll see you later, sweetie."

Debbie dropped back and fell into step beside Jake. "I've been wondering," she murmured. "Who, in all this crowd, is the Mr. Big, the one man Lucky's afraid of?"

"And have you worked it out?"

"I think I have. And it's the last person you'd expect."

"Yes," he said.

She stopped and faced him. "You, too?"

"I'm pretty sure. Who do you think?"

Debbie named a name and Jake nodded. "Spot on. It's the perfect cover."

"Perfect enough to fool us—for a while."

"That meeting should tell us. We've just got to listen in."

"Hey!" They looked up to find Brian on the path ahead of them. "Mr. Driver doesn't like being kept waiting. He sent me to say hurry up."

"And you always do what Mr. Driver tells you, don't you, Brian?" Jake observed.

Brian's face turned ugly. "Does that mean anything special?"

"It means exactly what it sounds as if it means," Jake said with a grin. "I reckon you've found your niche in life as Mr. Driver's errand boy."

Brian's fists balled. "You're asking for—"

"Brian." Lucky had turned to yell back at his henchman. "What the hell are you waiting for? Get over here."

"Yes, Mr. Driver."

Later that day Debbie slipped into the library and planted the bug under the table in the center. Before she could leave she heard the sound of footsteps about to enter. She shinnied quickly up the steps to take down a book and pretend to be looking at it.

"Hey, sweetie, what are you doing in here?" Lucky asked, coming in with Brian behind him.

"I was just looking for something to read," she told him. "I can read, you know, Lucky. I'm not just an airhead."

"Of course you're not. But you're neglecting our guests. Run along now."

She found Jake, gave him a swift thumbs-up sign and passed on without speaking. Soon people would be arriving for the big party and she must be at her best.

Despite his strenuous efforts Jake was unable to persuade Lucky to let him be present for the meeting. Once he'd seemed to be on the verge of relenting, but Brian had intervened, reminding him that his friends were nervous of strangers.

When the party was over, Jake, following Lucky's instructions, shepherded the guests away and wandered the grounds, looking for intruders. But under cover of darkness he slipped back into the house and up the stairs to Debbie's room.

"Thank goodness you're here," she said, letting him in. "I've been listening in, and they're planning a big delivery of drugs the day after tomorrow, at a place called 'The Greek's.' But I can't work out who the Greek is."

He went to the speaker to listen with her. The conversation was in full flow. "Any moment now we're going to discover if we're right about the brains behind all this," he murmured. "He's got to speak soon."

Suddenly they both tensed as they heard Lucky say, "Are those arrangements agreeable to you?"

And then came what they'd expected to hear—the thin, plaintive tones of Mr. Simpson. "Not entirely, Lucky. You've changed a few details, which, as you know, is something I dislike. Perhaps we'd better go over it again."

"Whatever you say, sir," Lucky replied.

At that little word "sir" Jake and Debbie turned to each other triumphantly. *"Yes,"* they said together.

In another moment they would have been in each other's arms, but Mr. Simpson's voice came again. "You're quite sure you understand what I want?"

Debbie and Jake exchanged an uncomfortable glance and the moment was gone. "That sweet little old man," Debbie said. "At first he had me completely fooled. He must have ordered Lucky to put him in that little attic room, to preserve his cover. No wonder Lucky went pale when I wanted to swap him with Rivers."

Jake made a wry face. "I guess you saw through him first."

"You don't really mean that."

"Why not? I can be fair."

"Jake—" she said in a voice of appeal.

"The meeting's breaking up," he said hurriedly. "I'd better get out of here quickly."

He was gone before she could say anything. Debbie looked at the closed door and the ache in her heart grew deeper. They were near the end of the job, and she had only a little time left to find a way through to him. There had never been a man she couldn't interest with her beauty and confidence, but now those very weapons had mysteriously turned against her. She shivered at the thought that she might not manage to turn Jake's heart back to her. The world had suddenly become very bleak.

Although the big meeting had broken up, Lucky spent the rest of the night talking to his minor associates and didn't try to trouble Debbie. Next morning her time was occupied saying goodbye to departing guests. She had a brief moment with Jake, who'd communicated their findings to Manners.

"He reckons 'The Greek's' is a restaurant called *The Athena,* moored on the Thames," he said. "They've had their suspicions about it, but this is the first hint of anything definite. They'll be watching it for the delivery. He told me to say that you'd done a marvelous job." He glanced over his shoulder. "I've got to go."

Debbie looked ahead to the coming two days, wondering if they'd bring her closer to Jake, or drive them apart forever. There was such a little time left, and she was so full of fear.

Then, without warning, everything changed dramatically. She said farewell to the last guest and was walking back to the house when a hand appeared from a bush and grasped her. The next moment she'd been pulled through the leaves and was confronting Jake. He was very pale. "I haven't much time," he said. "I have to be out of here in ten minutes."

"Lucky's sending you somewhere?"

"No, he's fired me."

"*What?* But why?"

"The crime was putting a dent in his precious Rolls, but there's something odd about the way it happened. As soon as I touched the car it shot forward into a wall. It had been tampered with."

"Who? Why?"

"My guess is Brian. As for why—there are two possibilities. One is that he's simply jealous and wants me out for his own reasons. The other is that he's seen through my cover."

"Then he'd tell Lucky, and Lucky would kill you, not fire you."

"Yes, but he might not want to do it here. There's too much going on here already. Anyway, I can't take the chance. I want you to leave with me."

"Why? They don't suspect me."

"We don't know that. I'm not leaving you here alone."

"Oh, yes you are. Don't start getting protective on me now, Stoneface. With you out of the way it's doubly important that I stay."

"Debbie," he said urgently. "I haven't time to argue. Get your things."

"Not a hope. You've got to admit I've done my job successfully so far."

"Up to a point, relying very heavily on what you look like in a gold lamé bikini," he snapped. It was unjust, but he was in a turmoil of fear for her and in no mood to guard his tongue.

"Oh, really?" she said crossly. "Then *you* try wearing a gold lamé bikini and see how far you get."

"Look, I didn't mean—"

"Go away, Jake. We've talked as long as it's safe."

"And suppose I go home and find someone waiting for me? I might not be able to get a warning to you."

"Then call Manners and get him to check your flat. Meanwhile, you can stay in mine."

"Right. That's not a bad idea."

"I won't give you the key because you don't need it," she reminded him wryly.

"But I still want you to come with me."

"No, no and no." She backed away from his outstretched hand. "I think Lucky's coming. Go quickly, Jake—and take care."

"You take care," he said somberly.

He let himself into her flat a few hours later. His first job was to call Manners to bring the chief up to date with developments. But Manners also had news for him. As he listened, Jake went deadly pale.

"How the hell did you let Danvers escape?" he exploded.

"He had some help," Manners said bitterly. "The van was attacked."

"But that means Lucky knows I didn't kill him. So by now he's worked out that I'm police, and Debbie's in danger. I'm going to get back there."

"Stay where you are," Manner snapped. "There's no reason to think he knows about her. If you go back you could be the thing that gives her away."

It was true but shivers went up Jake's spine at the thought of leaving Debbie to face her fate alone. "I'll be careful," he promised. "But I have to go."

"Listen," Manners said firmly, "I don't want you messing up my operation by any solo efforts. You stay right away. That's an order."

Jake came off the phone feeling sick. The little apartment around him was dreadfully quiet. At the same time it echoed with her presence. It was only a few days ago that they'd been there together, laughing and loving. And he'd blown the idyll apart with his suspicions. Now he might never see her again.

His head was throbbing painfully and he needed nothing so much as a stiff drink. He hunted around but Debbie didn't seem to approve of alcohol, for he found nothing.

Failing a drink he decided to look for some aspirin, but the bathroom cabinet was empty. He knew that if he let the headache take a real hold it would rapidly become unbearable, and began a determined search of the flat, opening drawer after drawer. He didn't find any aspirin, but he did find the enlarged photographs of their first meeting.

When the last guest had gone Lucky announced that they would stay there for a couple of days, and then he would be taking Debbie "somewhere special." Meanwhile he was busy on the phone and hardly had time to speak to her.

On the day when she knew the delivery was to be made at *The Athena,* Debbie spent most of the time in her room, hoping that Jake would risk calling her. At last the phone rang by her bed. She snatched it up quickly, but the voice was a woman's that she'd never heard before. "Are you Silver?" the woman asked.

"That's right."

"I've heard about you. They say you're Lucky's woman."

"Who is this?"

"Never mind my name. Do you know how I knew to come through to this particular phone?"

Debbie thought she could guess; she judged it safer to say, "I can't imagine."

"I thought not. You're too stupid. You have to be stupid to fall for Lucky. I was. That was my phone once. One day it'll be some other woman's."

"That's the luck of the draw," Debbie said cautiously.

The woman's voice grew hard. "There's no luck about it," she said bitterly. "It goes the way *he* wants. Oh, I expect you think you're having it all your own way right now, don't you? You've got him at your feet, flowers, gifts, abject devotion. And he actually likes it if you give nothing back—at least for a while. But it's only a game. He'll play it as long as he enjoys it, and then suddenly it's all over. If you're fortunate he'll take back all his gifts and throw you out on your ear. If you're not—" She left the implication hanging.

"Was that what happened to you?" Debbie asked. "Getting thrown out on your ear?"

"I escaped just in time. If I hadn't—well, I don't like to think."

Debbie decided to take a risk. "You're Liz James, aren't you?" she asked.

There was a silence. "I don't know what you mean."

"But you are."

"So what if I am?"

"A mutual friend of ours has been worried about you," Debbie said, picking her words with care. "You vanished so suddenly, he was afraid you'd met with an accident."

"I would have done if I hadn't vanished."

"He'll be glad to know you're all right."

"And who's going to tell him?"

"I might bump into him."

There was another long silence. "Are you ... the same as him? I mean, the same line of business?"

"Let's just say we're friends."

"I've got to go now."

"Look, just tell me where you are."

"It doesn't matter. Really it doesn't."

"Liz—*Liz*." But Debbie found herself talking to a dead line. Thoughtfully she replaced the receiver.

For a long time Jake stared at the photographs, his head ringing with the memory of George saying, "Debbie didn't want any pics. When she knew you weren't Speke she said they weren't of any interest."

But it hadn't been true. And Jake didn't need to be clairvoyant to know who'd been pulling George's strings. Debbie had told him to deny her interest, while all the time she'd been treasuring his image as much as he'd been treasuring hers.

The pictures were all good ones of himself, his eyes fixed intently on her in the fierce concentration of desire.

But there was one that showed her own face clearly and it made Jake go very still, his heart beating loudly at what that picture revealed.

If he'd been lost in desire, so had she. The woman in the picture was calculating nothing. Her expression was open, candid, absorbed in passion. No man could ask more than to see that face gazing up at him from his arms.

As if a signal had been given, the floodgates of his mind opened and memories—half noticed, half understood— burst through. The passionate anger that had swept him when he saw her bruise and believed Lucky had inflicted it. He'd congratulated himself on discovering the truth before he poured out his feelings and made a fool of himself. But he hadn't actually *discovered* the truth. She'd told him. What a laugh she could have enjoyed at all the tender, loving things that he'd almost said. But she'd headed him off.

His brain was crowded with images: Lucky prostrating himself before every trick Silver pulled off, and Silver enjoying the joke. Of course she knew how to make a fool of men. She had a genius for it.

But not with himself.

That was it. That was the difference between the way she treated Lucky and the way she treated him. And he'd yearned to find a difference. The very strength of that yearning should have warned him that he was on a dangerous road, where there were no signposts. Or perhaps there were, and he was the only man who couldn't recognize them.

She could have made him as big a clown as Lucky, but she'd refused to do so. Why? The answer to that was the answer to everything.

At their first lovemaking she'd given a tiny gasp as he'd entered her. He hadn't thought of it at the time but now it came back to him, and with it, the meaning. He wasn't the first man she'd lain with, but he was the first for some time. He looked around her austere bedroom and the knowledge came to him, with the force of certainty, that no other lover had entered this room in the two years she'd lived there. The men she'd worked with on the force had sighed their sighs and dreamed their dreams, but none of them had made it this far. Behind the siren surface was a deeply fastidious woman. And he, who prided himself on his insight, had understood precisely nothing.

She'd opened her arms to him with joyous abandon and the mistrustful streak in his nature had made him respond like a narrow-minded hick, incapable of responding to her generosity. Because of that he'd rejected her. She'd covered her hurt with a teasing laugh, but the hurt was there.

And now he found another memory coming to the surface, one he'd avoided, but which mustn't be dodged anymore because it told him so much about himself and his own fears. Patsy Selkirk, who'd died not knowing that he loved her, because he'd never said the words. They would have meant the world to her, but he'd said them only over her grave, when it was too late. And hated himself ever since.

Now there was Debbie, who meant a thousand times more to him. But he'd been ordered to abandon her when she was in danger, and once again it might be too late for all the things he needed to say.

Eleven

***

Lucky wouldn't tell Debbie where they were going, and she didn't let on that she knew anything about *The Athena*. As Brian drove them through the night Lucky seemed to be absorbed in his own thoughts. From time to time he drummed his fingers against the door. Debbie's attempts at conversation were met with grunts.

At last Debbie could make out some street lamps and saw they were in a small town. They drove through the deserted streets until the Rolls pulled up. She stepped out, feeling the chill air against her skin, and realized that they were by the river. Just ahead was moored a large boat, on which she could discern the name *The Athena*. "It's a restaurant," Lucky told her. "Of course it's closed for the night, but they opened for me."

He gave her his arm and she hobbled on board, hampered by her tight, ankle-length dress. She'd wanted to wear a velvet pantsuit that would have given her freedom of movement, but Lucky had insisted on the dress. On one side the boat was open to the town. On the other side it looked out onto the dark river. The water was quiet now, but Debbie saw how easy it would be for smaller boats to come upriver from the sea and deliver their cargo to *The Athena* without anyone being the wiser.

"Anything troubling you?" Lucky asked, looking at her intently.

"No, not a thing," she insisted, smiling brightly. Actually she'd been wondering where Jake was. Since Manners knew about this, Jake and the police should have been there, but there was no sign of him.

Lucky handed her gallantly below to where a table was laid for two. The crystal gleamed and champagne stood in a nearby cooler. He poured her a glass and toasted her, smiling. But the smile was dead, and now Debbie knew something was wrong.

"Drink up, sweetie," Lucky told her. "Let's toast our goodbye."

"Are we saying goodbye, Lucky?" she asked, trying to sound normal.

"Oh, yes. In your case, a very long and permanent goodbye. But before you go, why don't you tell me who you really are?"

"But you know who I am," she cooed winsomely, playing the part of a woman too stupid to understand him. "I'm Silver. *Your* Silver."

"That's what I thought. There aren't many people who've ever fooled Lucky Driver, and none that are alive to tell about it."

She made one last try, sashaying toward him and murmuring winsomely, "Lucky, sweetheart, why are you mad at me? I just don't understand a word you're saying."

He regarded her with chill malevolence. "I think you understand very well. You're police. You've been spying on me. You and your friend, *Jake*. Oh, yes, I know about him, too. *Liz* told me."

"Liz? Liz who?"

"Liz who, she asks. Liz James, a beautiful lady who's worth a hundred of you. We had a slight misunderstanding, but she's loyal to me. She called and told me about you—and Jake Garfield. I've taken care of him. Now I'm going to take care of you."

"Jake—" she whispered, drowning in horror.

Lucky grinned nastily. "It was smart for him to go to your flat instead of his own. But I'm even smarter. He's at the bottom of the river, wearing a pair of specially manufactured cement shoes."

She wanted to scream out her anguish. The love that had brightened her life had turned it to blackness in one terrible moment. Jake was dead and there was nothing left that mattered.

Nothing but hate. It was hate that gave power to the arm that she swung back and forward to land a stinging blow on Lucky's jaw. It sent him flying backward, crashing against the table, carrying it to the floor, where he landed and lay staring up at her with a look of astonishment. Debbie tried to follow through quickly but the narrow dress hampered her. Of course, Lucky had known. That's why he'd made her change. It was so easy to see now; that and her own stupidity in hinting the truth to Liz James. Jake had paid the price for that with his life, and now every fiber in her being was concentrated on the need to punish his killer.

Lucky was picking himself up. Debbie lunged for him but suddenly Brian was there, grabbing her and thrusting her hard against the bulkhead. His eyes were filled with pleasure at having got her at a disadvantage at last.

Lucky sounded mournful. "You really hurt me, Silver. I was crazy about you. And all you gave me was one lousy night."

"I didn't even give you that," she snapped. "I drugged your drink so that I wouldn't have to let you touch me, and you were too stupid to know the difference."

Lucky's face distorted. A loud cry broke from him and he lunged forward at her. Debbie's legs might be constrained but her arms were still free. The side of her hand across his nose sent him staggering back clutching his face. Quick as a flash she ran for it, stumbling up the steps, hearing Lucky's cry of, "After her!"

She made it to the deck but Brian was right behind her. He was heavy and strong but a clumsy mover. He managed to get hold of her but she ground her high heel against his ankle hard enough to make him howl, and managed to get her arms about him, imprisoning both his arms. The effort he put out to break her hold sent her flying back against the rail with such force that she went right over it.

She had enough wits left to take a deep breath before she hit the water to sink as deep as she dared. She came up slowly, kicking as hard as the tight dress would let her, to get along the boat, away from the spot where she'd fallen. At last her breath ran out and she was forced to surface, and to her relief she was some yards away. Lucky and Brian were at the rail, peering down into the dark water. Taking another breath, she sank below the surface again and managed to move along even farther. When she came up they were still looking down, and she heard Brian say, "Nothing. I reckon she sank in that dress."

"Good riddance! Okay, let's get back to work."

They turned away from the side. Debbie waited until they'd disappeared before she moved. Her heart was aching for Jake but she knew her grief must be suppressed until later. Her first duty was to get to shore and contact Chief Manners. She began to back off from the boat, but the waterlogged dress was a hindrance. She tried to kick but she couldn't move her legs properly and she felt herself being dragged down. She managed to make it back to the surface but it was like being trapped in a sack. With dread she felt herself going under again and thrashed about frantically.

Then, unbelievably, she collided with a human form, a hand went over her mouth and a voice in her ear said, "Don't make a noise."

"Jake!" she whispered in frantic joy. "They said you were dead."

"I nearly was. Tell you about it later. This way. We haven't much time."

He helped her to dog-paddle across the river to where a weeping willow hung down into the water by the far bank. A motor launch was moored under the shelter of the tree, and he helped her aboard.

"*Jake,*" she said again, and put her arms around him. For a moment the job was forgotten in the inexpressible joy of having him safe again. He held her close. "Lucky said he'd killed you," she murmured. "He said you were in the river in cement shoes. Oh, God, you're alive!" Tears poured down her face.

"They sent a man to your flat to kill me, but I was on my guard. He's in a cell right now. Manners promised to have a squad here tonight. I guess they haven't shown up yet. But then, neither has the delivery, so there's still time."

"Jake, I have to tell you. It was my fault our cover was blown."

"What do you mean?"

"Liz James called me at the house. She got away to another country."

"Well, thank heavens for that!"

"But I let on that I knew who she was. She must have worked the rest out and called Lucky to warn him about both of us. I could kick myself for slipping up like that—"

"Hey, it's all right. I made mistakes, too."

"But don't you see, maybe the delivery isn't happening tonight at all? If Lucky knows who you are he may have called it off."

"He hasn't had time. The plans are too elaborate to change at the last minute. Besides, he thinks he's safe. He doesn't know we listened in to the meeting. Who's on the boat?"

"I didn't see anyone but Lucky and Brian."

"Right. I'm going across. Stay here and keep your eyes skinned for any movement on the river."

He was back in the water before she could stop him. She tried to keep her eyes on him, but he swam quietly and in the darkness she'd soon lost him.

She sat there shivering with cold but also furious with herself. She wanted to be not only Jake's woman but also his comrade, fighting beside him. But she'd had to rely on him for rescue like some Victorian maiden. She could have screamed with vexation.

From this distance she could just make out *The Athena*, its lights gleaming across the water. Suddenly she heard a shout in the quiet night, then another, coming from the direction of the boat. She couldn't see anything but her instincts told her that something had gone wrong with

Jake. She looked frantically back down the river, and far off she could just discern some movement. But whether this was the delivery boats or Chief Manners with police reinforcements, she couldn't tell. Even if it were Manners, he would arrive too late to assist Jake. There was only one person who could do that. Stripping off her dress she dove into the water and swam back the way she'd come.

To her relief there was nobody near the side as she neared the boat. The ladder had already been lowered to the water, ready for the deliveries, and she crept noiselessly up it and over the rail.

She began to make her way noiselessly down through the boat, in the direction from which she'd come earlier. She stopped as she heard Lucky's voice coming from the saloon. She couldn't make out the words but she could tell by the tone that Lucky was pleased with himself. Her blood ran cold as she thought what that might mean. Then came Jake's voice, snapping with anger, and she breathed again. At least he was alive.

A white steward's jacket was hanging nearby. Her flimsy bra and panties were sodden and transparent, and she slipped the jacket on to cover herself from the chill night air, and crept on down the stairs. At last she could see the saloon door, standing open, and she could hear what Lucky was saying.

"You've really caused me more trouble than you're worth, but that's going to end now."

Debbie crept close enough to peer through the door. Brian was lying on the floor, apparently out cold, as if Jake had managed to overpower him. But Debbie could see Lucky standing there with a gun. Jake himself was out of sight, cut off by the angle of the door.

Debbie thought fast. She couldn't take Lucky by surprise because he had a clear view of the door through which she must enter. But perhaps there was another way...

Lucky was still talking. "I was sorry about what I had to do to Silver, but she got what she deserved...."

"Are you sure about that, Lucky?"

Debbie glided into the room and stood looking at him, one hand clutching the edges of the jacket together at her throat. Lucky's eyes flickered to her for a fraction of a second, but not long enough to give Jake a chance to jump him. "So you didn't drown after all," he said. "Never mind. I can finish you off now, just as easily."

Debbie assumed her most provocative smile. "Don't be so hasty, Lucky," she purred. "There's something you haven't taken into account."

"And what's that?" he sneered.

"This," she said simply, dropping the jacket to the floor and revealing her nearly naked body.

The result was all she'd hoped. Lucky paled and took a gasping breath. He fought for control but he couldn't tear his eyes from her quickly enough. In that split second Jake lunged forward, seized the hand holding the gun and forced it up, so that the bullet discharged into the ceiling. The next moment they were on the floor, wrestling back and forth until Jake ended it with one stunning punch.

Then he looked up at Debbie, and there was something in his eyes that made her heart sing.

"Thanks," he said briefly. But that was all she needed.

Shouts from outside sent them hurrying up the stairs to look over the railings. The water was full of boats, most of them police launches. Debbie could just make out Mr. Simpson, struggling between two officers. Manners emerged and climbed the ladder to the deck of *The Athena*. "Got the lot of them," he announced triumphantly. Then he scowled at Jake. "I don't know what the devil you think you're doing here, but you can tell me that later."

More policemen appeared over the rail. There seemed no end to them, swarming everywhere, taking charge. They brought Lucky and Brian up to the deck. Lucky looked at her with hate before being hauled away. But Debbie had no time for him. She was looking for Jake, longing to see in his eyes that their misunderstanding was over and they could begin again. Perhaps he would never say the words.

But Manners was monopolizing Jake. Someone wrapped a blanket around Debbie's shoulders and she turned her head to thank them. When she looked back there was no sign of Jake.

Twelve

The second letter infuriated Debbie even more than the first. In the first one the lawyer had merely stated that his client was interested in buying a partnership in her business and would she please state the price? The second one, ignoring her reply, flatly refusing to consider the idea, stated baldly that the client would call on her that afternoon to discuss terms. She'd telephoned the lawyer's office but it was a Saturday and he'd gone fishing.

Briefly Debbie considered going out herself. That would teach the unnamed client to consider other people before he simply announced his arrival. On second thought, she decided to stay in and tell him what she thought of him. It seemed a long time since she'd enjoyed a really satisfying bust-up. Not since...

Not since Jake. Two weeks had passed since Manners had scooped up Lucky, Brian, Mr. Simpson and all the rest. It had been a resounding triumph for everyone concerned and she'd received plaudits when she'd gone to the police station to make her statement. Everything would have been perfect, except that Jake had slid quietly out of her life. There'd been no grand parting. He just hadn't been there when she made her statement, and he hadn't called her. At last, swallowing her pride, she'd dropped in to see Manners to ask if there was anything further he wanted from her. He said not for the moment, and they enjoyed a coffee, during which she asked casually how Jake was doing.

"No idea," Manner said casually. "He left the force. I thought you'd have known."

It had hit her like a blow in the stomach. Despite their differences she hadn't believed he could simply walk off without a backward glance. Surely they'd been closer than that? She knew he'd distrusted her sexuality, but how could he maintain his distrust when she'd used that very sexuality to save his life?

But he'd simply brushed her aside without a word. She was left with the bitter and ironic realization that even their relationship had been a part of his act, demanded by the requirements of the job.

But with her it was different. In long cruel nights she faced the fact that for the first time she'd found a man to whom she could give her heart, wholly and without reserve. And he hadn't wanted it.

She'd told herself that she could easily have loved him, and then found what lovers have repeatedly discovered— that when you got to the point of saying "could have loved" it was already too late.

She'd known that her nickname at the station was Harker the Heartbreaker and she'd treated it as a cheerful game. How could it be anything else? She'd never known what heartbreak felt like. But now she was discovering. It meant waking every morning in a gray fog of fear because the life that stretched ahead was empty and barren, without the one person who mattered. Sometimes she awoke to find her pillow wet with tears that she couldn't remember shedding.

At three o'clock the doorbell rang and she opened it, braced for battle. But when she saw who was there she simply stood, openmouthed, disbelieving.

"May I come in?" Jake asked.

She pulled herself together. "Of course." She stepped back to let him pass. "The place is going to be crowded this afternoon. I'm also expecting someone who wants to buy into my business—such as it is."

"Has he offered a decent price?"

"About ten times what it's worth."

"Then take his money and run," Jake advised.

"What?"

"Lesson One in the Jake Garfield School of Life— when confronted by a sucker, don't hesitate. Take as much advantage of him as possible. I didn't expect to have to teach *you* that. You must be losing your touch."

She tried to speak lightly. "Maybe I'm not so sure of my touch as I once was."

He regarded her with raised eyebrows. "Is this the Debbie Harker I used to know? Come on, Debbie. If you lose your arrogance it'll be like the vanishing of a fixed point in the world. I'm not sure how I'd manage without it."

"Nobody's asking you to manage with it or without it," she informed him coolly.

"That's what I told myself," he agreed. "But some things happen to us whether we want them to or not. Haven't you discovered that? If you haven't, maybe I've wasted my time coming here."

Debbie stared. The possible implications of this speech were so tremendous that she did something she'd never done before in her entire life. She took fright. She panicked. She backed off.

"I— We would you like some coffee?" she stammered.

He didn't seem surprised by the way she ignored the gauntlet he'd tossed down. Perhaps he was biding his time. Or perhaps he understood about unexpected fear. "Thank you," he said gravely. "Coffee would be nice. And you can tell me about your business partner."

"He isn't my partner and he isn't going to be. Why should I want a man around, getting in my way, trying to change the way I do things?"

"Maybe he won't try. Perhaps he admires you and simply wants to work with you."

"Oh, indeed! And perhaps—" She eyed him narrowly. "Do you know who it is?"

He sighed. "You're being very stupid this afternoon, Debbie. Where's the razor-sharp intellect I'd looked forward to joining forces with?"

"You?" she said explosively.

"Didn't you ever guess it might be me?"

She should have thought of it long ago, but it hadn't crossed her mind. "Of course I didn't. Why should you do it this way when you could simply have approached me yourself?"

"I wanted to be businesslike. And that price is what I reckon your abilities are worth."

"My razor-sharp intellect," she echoed wryly.

"Well, as you once pointed out, you have certain talents that I lack. You even saved my life with them. I think we could make a great team." He made a wry face.

"You've got to let me join forces with you, Debbie. I'm out of a job."

"Manners told me you'd left the force. I couldn't understand it."

"I had to disobey a direct order to be at *The Athena* that night. I couldn't stay away when you were in danger. And I decided then and there that I was never again going to be in a position where someone could order me to abandon you to your fate. So I resigned."

"But *you* abandoned me, this last two weeks."

"Remember how you used to call me a coward, joking? But it's not a joke. I've thought I was so strong, but the truth is I was scared by the effect you've always had on me. You make the world a different place. You make me a different man, and I wasn't sure I was ready for that.

"But what scared me most was the thought that you might die without hearing me say that I loved you. When that night was over I thought it would be easy, but suddenly all my courage ran out of the soles of my feet. I've spent two weeks trying to summon up the nerve to approach you, and ask if you could manage to love me in return. I've put it off and put it off because the answer's so important. I can't go back to being the man I was before. I don't like him enough to want to do that."

"*If* I could manage to love you . . ." she echoed slowly in wonder. "Didn't you know that I loved you all the time?"

"I couldn't believe that. It would be too wonderful to be true."

"Then I'll have to convince you," she said, putting her arms about him.

She kissed him gently. This was no time for passion. On that level they already understood each other well. Now they had to discover how they stood with each other in a thousand other ways.

"Well?" she said at last.

"I think I'm beginning to understand," he said slowly. "You may have to explain it to me a lot. I can be very stupid sometimes."

"Yes," she said tenderly. "Yes, Stoneface, you can be very stupid."

"Stone face, stone heart," he said ironically. "That reputation has been useful to me, but it was never really true. I tried to make it true. I wanted a stone heart because it was the only way to resist you, and it didn't work. I'm here to abandon all my defenses and tell you that I I—"

She laid a hand over his mouth. "We don't need words."

"Yes, we do. Words matter. I love you, Debbie, and I want your love in return. Fair exchange."

She smiled. "All right. Fair exchange. But are you sure you won't start being suspicious of me again?"

"On the contrary, I'm sure I will. You're a suspicious character. You and your two faces. But as far as I'm concerned, you can have a thousand faces."

"I do have a thousand faces."

"It doesn't matter," he said firmly, lowering his head to hers. "I love every last one of them."

* * * * *

It's a celebration of motherhood...

Three Mothers & a Cradle

Silhouette's special collection dedicated to motherhood will touch your hearts this spring.

Take one very special baby cradle, carved long ago with tenderness and care...
Add the talent of three award-winning authors...
And you get three fantastic romances for you to treasure.

Debbie Macomber | *Rock-A-Bye-Baby*
Jill Marie Landis | *Cradle Song*
Gina Ferris Wilkins | *Beginnings*

Available: February 1996
Price: £4.99

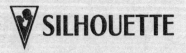 SILHOUETTE

SILHOUETTE

Desire

COMING NEXT MONTH

WILDCAT
Rebecca Brandewyne

Man of the Month

Morgan McCain hadn't wanted a new partner, but he couldn't afford to buy Cat Devlin's shares. So he was going to have to live with her and like it!

A WOLF IN THE DESERT
BJ James

Men of the Black Watch

Matthew Winter Sky had rescued Patience O'Hara from a gang of lawless drifters, but he knew she was jeopardizing the success of his mission. What could he do with her now he had her?

THE COWBOY TAKES A LADY
Cindy Gerard

When Sara Stewart propositioned him, sexy rancher Tucker Lambert surprised both of them by turning her down. Almost any man would have done, Sara hadn't really wanted *him* and, for the first time, that was important to Tucker.

SILHOUETTE

Desire

COMING NEXT MONTH

A WIFE IN TIME
Cathie Linz

Spellbound

Somehow Susannah Hall and Kane Wilder had been
transported back in time and were posing as man and wife.
Susannah had old-fashioned values, while Kane was wrestling
with old-fashioned lust…

THE BACHELOR'S BRIDE
Audra Adams

Rachel Morgan was having a baby by a wealthy, powerful
man—a man she couldn't even *remember*! A man who
wanted to be her husband!

THE ROGUE AND THE RICH GIRL
Christine Pacheco

Nicole Jackson hired Ace Lawson to take her where she
needed to go, but she hadn't planned on being stuck with him.
He might be able to teach her about life, although he knew
nothing about true love…

GET 4 BOOKS AND A MYSTERY GIFT

Return this coupon and we'll send you 4 Silhouette Desires and a mystery gift absolutely FREE! We'll even pay the postage and packing for you.

We're making you this offer to introduce you to the benefits of Reader Service: FREE home delivery of brand-new Silhouette romances, at least a month before they are available in the shops, FREE gifts and a monthly Newsletter packed with information.

Accepting these FREE books and gift places you under no obligation to buy, you may cancel at any time, even after receiving just your free shipment. Simply complete the coupon below and send it to:

SILHOUETTE READER SERVICE, FREEPOST, CROYDON, CR9 3WZ.

No stamp needed

Yes, please send me 4 free Silhouette Desires and a mystery gift. I understand that unless you hear from me, I will receive 6 superb new titles every month for just £2.20* each postage and packing free. I am under no obligation to purchase any books and I may cancel or suspend my subscription at any time, but the free books and gifts will be mine to keep in any case. (I am over 18 years of age)

1EP6SD

Ms/Mrs/Miss/Mr _____

Address _____

_____

_____ Postcode _____